FIREBOY

PRAISE FOR FIREBOY

"Fireboy is a story jam-packed with mystery, action, humour and surprises. You'll never look at science class or elementals the same way."

ARTHUR SLADE, GOVERNOR GENERAL'S
AWARD-WINNING AUTHOR OF *DUST*

"A gripping read! . . . Sam's engaging narrative voice in Fireboy is certain to draw readers into this mystery in which things are far from what they appear to be, and Sam herself is plunged deeper and deeper into mortal danger. Highly recommended!"

ALISON LOHANS, AWARD-WINNING
AUTHOR OF MORE THAN THIRTY BOOKS
FOR YOUNG READERS AND ADULTS

"'There comes a time in every girl's life when she really wishes she'd thought to pack wire cutters.' If that line made you laugh, or even smile slightly, Fireboy is for you! . . . The plot is quite exciting and kept me rapidly turning pages . . . an enjoyable book all around."

L. JAGI LAMPLIGHTER, AUTHOR OF *THE
BOOKS OF UNEXPECTED
ENLIGHTENMENT*

FIREBOY

SHADOWPAW
PRESS

EDWARD WILLETT

FIREBOY

Published by
Shadowpaw Press
Regina, Saskatchewan, Canada
www.shadowpawpress.com

Trade Paperback ISBN: 978-1-998273-42-3
Ebook ISBN: 978-1-998273-43-0

Cover art by Dwayne Wingert

Shadowpaw Press is grateful for the financial support of Creative Saskatchewan.

CONTENTS

CHAPTER 1
I SEE A FAMILIAR FACE

I knew things were getting weird when I saw my best friend's face in the campfire. I didn't realize *how* weird until the campfire followed me home.

Yeah, I know how that sounds. I can hear your mom whispering right now, "Back away slowly from the crazy girl, and when I give the signal, run for dear life!"

Probably that's what I should have done. Run for dear life. Or at least closed my blinds and hidden under the covers. But instead, when I saw that flicker of flame in the woods behind the barn, I sneaked downstairs, shoved on some shoes, put a poncho over my pyjamas, and went out into the rain to get a closer look.

My name is Samantha Anastasia MacReady: Sam for short. I'm thirteen years old and am in Grade 8 at Engelmann Middle School in the not-so-thriving metropolis of Limberpine, Alberta. And honest, I promise I'm not a crazy girl. Sure, I was a little freaked out the night my friend's face showed up in the fire—but I was freaked out anyway.

See, school was supposed to start in a few days, and that

meant I would be taking Dr. Ballard's Grade 8 science class, and that felt seriously weird because I was one of only two survivors of Dr. Ballard's Grade 7 science class.

The grown-ups called it "The Tragedy," complete with capital letters, in a whisper, at least when I was around— they seemed to think if they didn't talk about "The Tragedy" out loud, I might not remember that a bunch of my friends—including my *best* friend—had vanished into thin air.

It happened last May. While I was spending some quality time in the bathroom puking up everything I'd eaten since Grade 3, courtesy of a bad burrito, the other twenty members of my Grade 7 science class piled into a small school bus and headed up Mount Mollard for an overnight camping-trip-and-astronomy-adventure.

But they never reached the campground. The police found the bus lying on its side ten metres off the road. Dr. Ballard, still buckled into the driver's seat, was out cold. So was Meg Leblanc, who had only started at the school after Christmas and I'd hardly ever said two words to. She turned up at the back of the bus, buried in sleeping bags.

Every other kid had disappeared without a trace. Literally. Not so much as a footprint—weird because the ground was muddy. Even weirder, all their stuff was still in the bus—even their cellphones, and since most of them took their cellphones everywhere, including into the bathroom, that seemed a sure sign of foul play.

A busload of kids vanishing under mysterious circum-stances is like catnip to cable news. It had everything! Pathetic parents. Sobbing siblings. Valiant volunteers. Hovering helicopters. For days, Limberpine crawled with camera crews from CBC and Global and CTV and Fox and

CNN and ABC and NBC and networks I'd never heard of. I think the Home Shopping Network turned up at one point.

Anchorpersons in heavy makeup prowled the streets like bears trawling a mountain path for unwary hikers. I don't think anybody in town escaped being interviewed—not even me, but after I said a bunch of words thirteen-year-old girls aren't supposed to say on television and tried to kick the anchor-thing, they left me alone. (Meg Leblanc didn't kick anybody, as far as I know, but all they ever got out of her were grunts and monosyllables, so pretty soon they left her alone, too.)

After about ten days, the media frenzy fizzled out. Some celebrity announced she was either marrying or divorcing another celebrity—I forget which—and just like that, we were Old News.

The rest of the world moved on. We couldn't. We were stuck with what had happened and had to try to deal with it. I mostly dealt with it by moping and throwing things and binge-watching anime. That's probably why Dad decided he needed to get us both out of the house.

"We'll go camping," he said. "Up at Lake Stickleback. It'll be fun."

So we went camping. It wasn't fun. It was cold. It started raining before we even had our tents up. And the campground didn't even have an outhouse.

Did I mention it was cold? And raining? Nothing says "having a good time" like trying to pee behind a bush in the woods when your goosebumps have goosebumps, and there's something rustling in the bushes.

I was tempted to steal Dad's truck, figure out how to drive it (how hard could it be?), and head home the minute we got there, but apparently, the great province of Alberta thinks twelve-almost-thirteen is too young to drive. (How unfair is that?) So I was stuck until Dad agreed we should go home. Which he didn't. He thought we would bond through shared misery. I don't know if we bonded, but we definitely mildewed.

Thankfully, it was only for two nights. The second day, it stopped raining, at least, although since the sun didn't come out and the fog lingered, it didn't exactly warm up or dry out. Fortunately, even though the campground was an outhouse-free zone, it had dry firewood stored in a shed, so at least we were able to get a fire going. Sitting around it that second night roasting hot dogs and marshmallows, I almost convinced myself I was having fun . . . right up until I remembered that my friends had never gotten the chance to sit around *their* campfire last spring. Suddenly, the marshmallows didn't taste as sweet.

That night, I had trouble sleeping, like I had all summer. When I finally dozed off, I woke up almost right away because I thought I heard someone call my name.

Sam?

It was barely a whisper.

"Dad?" I said—softly because I wasn't sure, and I didn't want to wake him up if I'd just been dreaming.

I didn't hear my name again. Instead, I heard something else—the crackle of fire. And I could see it, too, an orange, flickering glow through the thin nylon of my tent.

I scrambled out of my sleeping bag and stuck my head out through the tent flap.

Our campfire was blazing, flames jumping four feet in the air, and that was wrong because I'd seen Dad put it out and stir the ashes before we'd gone to bed.

And then I heard my name again, only this time I knew

where it was coming from—not from the direction of Dad's tent, but from the campfire.

It's a dream, I thought.

But I could smell smoke and feel the heat on my face and the ground pressing into my knees. I crawled out, and when I stood up, the knees of my pyjamas were wet, and my bare feet were cold in the dewy grass.

Heart pounding, I approached the fire, step by slow step. The flames died down as I got closer. I looked down into the fire pit . . .

. . . and that's when I saw the face. It looked like a mask made of glass and filled with flames, but I recognized it instantly all the same.

It was the face of my best friend, Lorenzo.

There was no way I *wouldn't* know his face. We used to live side by side on the same street. We'd known each other since we learned to walk. We played together in each other's backyard. We started school together, did homework together, spent our summers together.

Then, when I was eight, Mom got sick, and she never got better. She died when I was nine, and Dad moved us out to a new house (new to us, it's at least a hundred years old) right on the edge of town because he couldn't bear to keep living in the old house anymore.

Neither could I.

Even after we moved, though, I saw Lorenzo all the time because Limberpine isn't big. As in *really* not big. You can bicycle anywhere in ten minutes, and of course, we were still in the same school and the same grade. So we kept being best friends, right through elementary school, and into middle school, and . . .

. . . and he had been on the bus last May.

I stared at his fiery face. He stared back. His lips moved, and I thought I heard my name again, but I couldn't make out anything else, just the crackle and whisper of flame.

Then his eyes got wide, and his mouth opened wide, and he screamed, a high-pitched hissing sound, like the sound of sap sizzling in a log in the fire, and I screamed, too. "Lorenzo!"

And then, suddenly, Dad was beside me, pouring a bucket of water on the fire, and Lorenzo's face disappeared with the rest of the campfire in a cloud of steam . . . but I thought I heard him screaming a second or two longer in the hissing vapour.

Furious, I yelled at Dad, "Why'd you do that?"

He couldn't figure out why I was upset. I stormed back into my tent, and I'm not ashamed to say I cried in my pillow, although, unfortunately, I didn't cry myself to sleep. I stayed awake almost all the rest of the night, which didn't help my mood in the morning. Especially since, by then, it had started raining again.

We drove home in surly silence and ate in grumpy gloom, and I went to bed early.

I was sure I'd fall asleep the minute I lay down. My bed's *way* comfier than a sleeping bag on the ground, and the last two nights' sleep had been lousy. But I couldn't. In my head I kept seeing what I'd seen the night before, like I was watching a YouTube video over and over. Hearing my name. Leaving the tent. Lorenzo's face in the fire. And then his terrible scream . . .

I dozed off at last, but every few minutes, I'd wake up and roll over. I'd hit my pillow with my fists to plump it up. Then I'd flip it over to get the cool side. Then I'd doze off, wake up, and do it again.

I was doing it for about the twelfth time when I suddenly realized that the wall of my room was flickering with orange light. *Firelight.* Just like the light that had flickered on my tent walls the night before.

I scrambled out of bed, caught my foot in the covers, fell with a thump, fought my way free, and finally reached the window. Flames danced in the woods, out past the old barn where Dad stores his beloved (but rusty) 1967 Mustang GT. A campfire, it looked like, but nobody camps in the thick woods at the base of Mount Mollard, and certainly not by our barn. Nothing should be burning out there unless the forest was on fire, and it clearly wasn't.

For one thing, it was still drizzling rain.

Sam?

I yelped and spun toward the door, thinking Dad had heard me fall and come to check on me. But there was nobody there.

Sam?

The voice—*Lorenzo's* voice—was only in my head.

Maybe last night's voice had only been in my head, too.

I'm not crazy, I told myself fiercely.

Of course not, myself answered. *Not crazy at all. Just seeing things and hearing things. And talking to yourself.*

I told myself to shut up.

Maybe if I'd been smart enough to tell myself it was a dream, smart enough to jump back into bed, I would have fallen asleep. If I had, I probably never would have seen the fire again . . . or heard Lorenzo's voice again.

Instead, two minutes later, I was heading out the back door, the rain pattering on my poncho, that impossible fire still flickering in the woods ahead of me . . . and still calling my name.

Sam . . . Sam!

CHAPTER 2
I MEET A HOT BOY

As I walked through the drizzle across the wet grass, the fire grew clearer—and weirder. The tips of the leaping flames were level with my eyes! Any ordinary fire shooting five feet into the air in the trees behind our barn would have set the woods on fire by now, rain or no rain, but this one just stood there, in one place, like a pillar . . .

. . . no, like a *person*!

I suddenly realized that's what I was seeing—a person made of fire!—and my heart leaped, and I broke into a run because I recognized this burning boy, from the way he stood, from the way he was looking at me, from a million different things.

Lorenzo!

I wanted to throw my arms around him, but that seemed like a really, really bad idea since I could feel the heat radiating off him from ten feet away and hear the raindrops sizzling on his hot . . . um . . . skin? I skidded to a halt in the wet grass and stared at him. My pulse pounded in my ears. "Lorenzo?" I whispered.

His face still looked like a glass mask filled with fire. The rest of his body was less distinct, legs and arms and torso just kind of suggested by the swirl of flame and smoke, which was probably just as well since for obvious reasons, he wasn't wearing clothes.

"Sam! At last!" It was Lorenzo's voice, but distorted, hissing and crackling like Dad's old vinyl records.

Dad! I shot a nervous glance over my shoulder. If Dad saw a fire out behind the barn, he'd come rushing out with another bucket of water. "Can you move?" I asked Lorenzo.

"Yes. Why?"

"We need to get out of sight of the house. This way."

I hurried a few feet to my right, fire-Lorenzo gliding across the ground behind me, putting the black bulk of the barn between us and the house's dark windows. The light of his burning body made my shadow dance behind me on the barn wall. I finally asked the all-important question. "What happened to you?"

"I don't know," he said after a moment.

I stared at his flaming face. "What do you mean, you don't know? How can you not know how you turned into a walking campfire?"

"I mean, I don't know how he did it," Lorenzo said.

"Who?"

"I don't know."

This was getting us nowhere. "Do you remember what happened to the bus?"

"Kind of. I was looking at my phone. I felt the bus start to tip over. Everyone was screaming. After that . . . it's a blank."

"Did you hit your head?"

"I don't think so."

"And when you woke up, you were all . . . um . . . flamey?"

"No. When I woke up, I was in a bed. And locked up in a room."

"Like a cell?"

"More like a dorm room. There's a desk and a chair and it has its own little bathroom with a sink and a toilet and a shower."

"A dorm room?" I blinked. "It's a school? Any idea where?"

"No. There aren't even any windows."

"Is that where you are right now?"

"Yes," he said. His fiery face scrunched up. "My parents must think I'm dead."

"They think you're missing," I said firmly. "Nobody knows what happened to any of you." *But yeah, they think you're dead.* I didn't say that out loud. Lorenzo probably felt bad enough. Or maybe he didn't feel anything at all. How did that work, exactly, without glands and a brain and all that other gooey inside-the-body stuff? "So what happened after you woke up?"

"I banged on the door. I shouted. I could hear other kids shouting and screaming, but faintly—we couldn't talk to each other. I lay back down. I . . . I cried. Eventually, I fell asleep again. I woke up when the door opened. A man came in. He was wearing a lab coat and a mask, but not a surgical mask."

"Then what kind was it?"

"More like a hockey goalie mask. It covered his whole face."

"A goalie mask?" I'd streamed an old horror movie called *Friday the Thirteenth* when I was nine when Mom was in the hospital and Dad was with her. (Without telling Dad, natch. He never would have let me. He would have had a point: I had nightmares for a week about being chased by a killer in a goalie mask.)

Lorenzo nodded. "All I could see was the glint of his eyes."

"What did he say?"

"Nothing." Fire-Lorenzo shuddered, flames dancing as though in a strong breeze, though not a breath of air stirred the leaves around us. A brief flash lit the clouds, and a few seconds later, thunder grumbled. The drizzle had almost stopped, but another storm would arrive soon.

"Nothing?" What kind of useless villain didn't lay out his whole plan to his victim in excruciating detail?

"No. He just walked over to the bed. That's when I found out it had straps on it. He strapped me down. I tried to struggle, but he was too strong.

"Then, he reached out and touched my head. And then . . ." His voice faded, and his flames, too, so for a moment, he looked no brighter than a dying coal in our fireplace. "It felt like he was pulling my insides out through my ears," he said at last, his voice little more than the crackling whisper of a burning twig.

"It hurt?"

"Not exactly. It was just . . . weird. Wrong. Kind of . . . disgusting. Like I'd touched something slimy. Like that day at the pond."

I remembered that. We'd gone swimming in a pool at the base of Mount Mollard, formed by a stream tumbling down the rocks from up above. Lorenzo had suddenly started shrieking and splashed out of the pool like he was being chased by a . . . well, by a killer in a goalie mask. He said he'd stepped on something awful.

Turned out it was a dead something-or-other. With fur. We couldn't really recognize it.

We stuck to the town swimming pool after that.

"I don't know how long it went on. When it finally stopped, the man unstrapped me and then walked out without saying a word. And I ran into the bathroom and threw up." His voice dropped even lower, so low I had to strain to hear it. "But a few hours later, he came back and did it again. And again, a few hours after that. And again after that. And the . . . fourth time, maybe? Or fifth? . . . it was different. All that awful sick-making sliminess stopped, and suddenly, I was . . ." He gestured at his burning body. "Like this. Standing in the corner of the room. Only for a minute or two. Then I was back in my real body. The man got up, nodded, unstrapped me, and walked out again." He sighed. "And I threw up again."

"And in between, he just . . . left you there? What about food?"

"There's also a woman," Lorenzo said. "She wears a lab coat, too, and a mask, but just an ordinary surgical mask, you know, like people wore during the pandemic. She brings food. Mostly sandwiches, baloney or ham, mainly. Chips. An apple or banana. A piece of cheese. A couple of bottles of water."

"Couldn't you try to escape when she comes in?"

Lorenzo shook his head. "She doesn't open the door unless I'm standing on the far side of the room. She puts the tray just inside the door, and I have to leave it there when I'm done."

I couldn't speak. Lorenzo carried on. "Anyway. The man

kept coming back, doing . . . whatever he did. I'm almost got used to it. I quit throwing up. And every time he did it, I was like *this* for longer."

"Couldn't you have . . . done something to him? I mean, you're the Human Torch!"

"He . . . controls me. Or at least keeps me from doing anything he doesn't want me to. It's hard to explain. It's like a —a pressure. In my head."

"But . . ." I stared at him. "Then how are you here?"

"As I began staying this way longer, I started noticing things I didn't the first time. One was a . . . a line of fire. In my head. Stretching from me to . . . well, I didn't know. I just knew I could follow it if I could get free. But that pressure he put on me . . . I couldn't do anything while he was in the room. I could only move if he allowed me to move, and all he would allow me to do was walk around the room.

"But I got to thinking: if *he* could turn me into whatever I am, maybe I could do it myself. And since I had nothing else to do, I started trying.

"At first, I couldn't make it happen. I couldn't get the knack of it. But then, all of a sudden, after he hadn't been in for a couple of days, I felt this kind of . . . *click*, I guess? . . . inside my head, and suddenly there I was, burning, standing in the corner of the room, looking at my unconscious body— and at that line of fire in my head. I kind of took hold of it, and when I did, I suddenly realized that *you* were at the other end. So I followed it. And the next thing I knew, I was in your campfire."

Lightning flashed again; the thunder followed much sooner this time. The wind hissed in the trees and plucked at my hair. It began to drizzle, then to rain again in earnest. Lorenzo almost vanished behind clouds of steam. I pulled the poncho tighter around my pyjama-clad body and folded my arms over my chest to keep it in place. I was glad of Lorenzo's heat: my front was warm, but my back was freezing. "And I'm the only one you have this . . . this 'line of fire' to?"

"Yes," Lorenzo said.

"But why were you just a face in the fire? Why weren't you a complete body, like now?"

"I think I was too far away from my real body up in the mountains. Only part of me was there. I tried to talk to you, but then someone poured a bucket of cold water all over me, and just like that, I was back in my real body."

I winced. "Dad. Sorry about that."

"Tonight, I finally got another chance. I followed the thread again, but I stopped myself out here. I didn't want to set your house on fire." His flames flickered, and his voice faded again to a crackling whisper. "I don't know how much longer I can stay. My body eventually pulls me back. I can feel it pulling me now. And the rain is starting to put me out."

Panic rose in me. "But I don't know what to do! How do I help you?"

"Find me. The *real* me. My real body. Find me. Free me. The man . . . he's started forcing me to stay outside of my body longer than I want to. I think . . ." His flames dimmed to a dull red glow. " . . . I'm *sure* that someday, maybe soon, he's going to be able to keep me out of my body permanently. If he does that . . . I think my real body will die, and I'll be like this forever. And if I lose my real body . . . how long will I still be *me*? How long will I still be Lorenzo?"

"Let me get Dad," I said. "He'll know what to—"

"No!" Lorenzo's flames brightened, and his voice strengthened, almost roared. "He'll go to the police or tell someone, and if the man found out, he'd either make me this way permanently or kill me trying to do it. I'm sure of it."

"What about the other kids? Is he doing this to them, too?"

"I don't know," Lorenzo said. "I still hear kids yelling, but I can't make out any words. Maybe some of the others can talk to each other, but . . ." In the rain, his fire body hissed like an angry cat. The momentary brightness had already faded, and so had his voice. "I can't stay much longer!" he whispered. "Sam, promise you'll help me—all of us. Promise!"

"But how do I even start?" I cried.

"Did anyone make it back from the wreck?" Both his flames and his voice had almost vanished now. I had to strain to make out his hissing, crackling words.

"Mr. Ballard," I said. "And Meg. Meg LeBlanc."

"Ask them," Lorenzo said. "Ask them what happened. Maybe they saw . . . *aaaaaah!*" His cry sounded no louder than a mosquito's buzz. He reached out to me with his burning, steam-wreathed arms. I flinched back—I couldn't help it— and then he collapsed in on himself, like a candle flame being snuffed, and just like that, he was gone.

But he wasn't *really* gone. Maybe none of the kids were.

My heart pounded in my chest as I stared at the place he had stood. Then and there, I made up my mind: whatever it took, I would get Lorenzo back!

If I didn't catch pneumonia. The rain suddenly became a downpour, and my poncho, it turned out, leaked. In seconds, I was soaked to the skin, my pyjamas clinging to me like wet toilet paper.

I dashed back to the house, bare feet splashing on the soaked lawn. Shivering in my bedroom, I stripped off the sodden pyjamas, pulled on a flannel nightgown I usually only wore in winter, and burrowed under my covers. Just in time: I heard Dad's door open and the click of a light switch. A bright band of illumination sprang to life beneath my bedroom door. A second later I heard it ease open. But I had my eyes closed and did my best to impersonate a soundly sleeping kid until the door clicked closed once more.

A minute later, it wasn't an impersonation.

CHAPTER 3
I HOLD A PRESS CONFERENCE

I jerked awake in the morning to the sound of Dad tripping over the wet pyjama lump I'd left in the middle of the floor—not the thud of his foot hitting the floor as he caught himself, but the sound of what he said afterwards. They were not the words he usually used to get me up in the morning.

I would have moved the pyjamas if I'd had any idea he was going to wake me up: it was still summer vacation, and so I'd figured I'd get to sleep in. Apparently not.

Dad took a deep breath after his first colourful exclamatory statement and then said, "Sam?"

"Mmmm?" I said, pretending I was just then waking up.

"Why are there wet pyjamas in the middle of the floor? Did you go outside in the rain?"

"I thought I saw something in the backyard," I said. "I'm sorry I didn't pick them up—"

"What did you think you saw?"

My missing best friend? Made out of fire? I imagined saying. But I only imagined it. In fact, fire in general didn't seem like something I should mention after the flare-up of the campfire up at Lake Stickleback. Dad hadn't said anything, but I think he suspected I'd poured kerosene on it or something.

"Some sort of animal in the trees," I said. And then I winced. Because I knew what was coming next.

I was right. "Sam, look at me."

I rolled over and blinked at his frowning face. "What?"

"An animal in the woods could be anything," Dad said sternly. "It could be a bear. A wolf. A cougar. It could be rabid. Or it might not be an animal at all. It might be somebody up to no good. It's not safe to leave the house in the middle of the night."

"I'm sorry," I mumbled. "It didn't look like a big animal. I thought maybe it was somebody's pet who was . . ."

"You didn't think at all," Dad snapped. "You never do."

That's not fair, I thought, but again, I didn't say it out loud, which is *proof*, when you think about it, that it *wasn't* fair and that I *do* think before I do things.

Sometimes, anyway. "I *said* I'm sorry."

Dad ran a hand over his chin. He'd shaved, which meant he was probably going out; he usually didn't bother if he was planning to be home all day. He'd grown a beard once, but Mom had made him . . .

My breath caught in my throat. I didn't want to think about Mom just then.

"I've got a job interview," Dad said. "Will you be all right?"

I sat up, suddenly excited. "Sure! A job interview? Where?"

"Brad's Auto. One of his mechanics quit, so Brad gave me a call. He knows how good I am with cars." Dad took a deep breath. "I've got a good feeling about this, Sam. I think the job's mine if I want it."

"Dad, that's terrific!" And it was. We'd been getting by on Dad's odd jobs and Mom's life insurance, but I knew how worried Dad was about money. We owned the old house free and clear, but there were still taxes to be paid and food to be bought and clothes for me and . . . well, there wasn't much money left over for anything else. Sometimes, there wasn't *any* money left over.

I knew I'd have to work every summer I was in high school if I wanted to go to college. But I hadn't even started Grade 8 yet, so aside from mowing the occasional lawn or a little babysitting, there wasn't much I could do to help right now. *Except maybe not worrying Dad by sneaking out into the rain in the middle of the night,* I thought guiltily.

Or, at least, not letting him find out about it. I'd been an idiot to leave my pyjamas lying on the floor.

"I'll be out until afternoon at least. What do you have planned?"

"Oh, you know . . . lazy summer stuff. I'll probably bike downtown."

"All right," Dad said. "But take your phone and be careful. Text me if you need anything."

"I will, Dad." I gave him my best smile. "Good luck!"

"Thanks." He smiled back. Then he picked up the wet pyjamas and tossed them at me. They splatted on my face, and I spluttered in shock. He laughed and went out.

There was no going back to sleep after being hit on the nose by wet pyjamas. I got up and got dressed and got on with my day . . . which wasn't at *all* the day I'd had planned before Lorenzo-the-Human-Torch had popped up behind the barn.

Ask Dr. Ballard and Meg, Lorenzo had said. Which made sense: maybe they knew what had happened, or had seen something, or . . . something.

The police had said the accident wasn't Dr. Ballard's fault. They said something had torn up the pavement before the bus came along, and that's why the bus crashed. So Dr. Ballard hadn't been arrested or run out of Limberpine. Some people had thought he'd probably leave anyway since he'd managed to misplace most of his Grade 7 science class, but the school had announced he was returning. The trouble was, I didn't know where he lived, and the phone book was no help: no listing.

However, I *did* know where Meg lived, not far from the abandoned railroad track that cut through the heart of town, in one of a row of run-down houses. Before Dad had bought our old farmhouse, he'd looked at renting one of them, but had changed his mind when he'd found out they were owned by some out-of-town landlord nobody ever seemed to see in person.

Well, the plethora of mouse droppings and dead cockroaches inside the one he'd looked at hadn't helped, either.

Forty-five minutes after I got a face-full of wet pyjamas, I was sitting on my bike, staring at Meg's place.

Our house was older, but hers *looked* older. It was smaller, too: one storey, just a box with two porches, one front, one back. The front porch roof sagged as though the square pillars holding it up were just too tired to stand up straight anymore. The house had once been blue, but most of the paint had peeled away, so now it was a grey house with blue acne. Scraggly bushes clawed at the walls as though trying to get in. Of the three windows facing me, two were cracked, and one (probably belonging to the bathroom, from the size of it) framed a piece of green garbage bag instead of glass. Chicken wire fenced a backyard where the weeds looked tall enough to get lost in. It was pretty much the saddest house I'd ever seen, but that wasn't what kept me from going up, knocking on the door, and asking for Meg.

No, what kept me in place was the white van parked in front of the house. A waving Canadian flag covered the side. Across it, black capital letters spelled out CALGARY EYEWITNESS NEWS. Across the bottom of the flag, black script edged in bright silver read, "If we don't see it happen, it's not news!"

"That makes no sense at all," I muttered.

The last thing I wanted was to cross paths with a vanload of vultures . . . I mean, reporters. For some reason, they'd come back to town, probably because school was going to start soon, giving them an excuse to revisit the Case of the Missing Science Class. I don't know what they thought they'd learn that was new. I mean, back when this all started, they'd not only interviewed everyone who knew anything about what had happened, they'd interviewed everyone who *didn't* know anything about what had happened, with special attention to anyone who didn't know anything about what had happened but had a crackpot conspiracy theory about it anyway.

Whyever they'd come back to town, the Eyewitness Ghouls in the van clearly hoped to waylay Meg, The Girl Who Lived—as some newsy had predictably dubbed her the minute the story broke. If she'd had a distinctive scar on her forehead, the reporters would have wet themselves on-camera, but alas, although Meg had probably hit her head since she'd been out cold, the blow had left no scar. Also, for the reporters to conjure *Maximus Pottermonium* they would have needed a Voldemort, and so far, they'd come up empty in the search for a He Who Must Not be Named, Devourer of Science Classes, Dr. Ballard having been cleared of wrongdoing.

I, on the other hand, had a lead: the masked man holding Lorenzo captive and, somehow, turning him into a flamesicle.

No way was I going to tell any reporters about him, though. Even if they believed me—which they wouldn't—what would a creepy dude like that do if he realized people were looking for him? Let all the kids go?

Not on their lives. Literally.

And then I thought, *You're stalling, Sam.* Which I was because I didn't have a plan.

The question was, how could I find out if Meg was inside her house without making the Calgary evening news?

My eyes traced the tree-and-bush-lined alley to Meg's wobbly-looking backyard fence, almost hidden behind the weeds, and I smiled. There could have been a marching band behind the house, and I wouldn't have been able to see it.

Which meant nobody in the van could, either.

I pushed off and rode down the street. As I passed the van, I glared at the driver, who was sucking on a cigarette, smoke drifting out through the open window. He glanced at me, and I gave him a one-fingered salute. Then I pedalled off as if I thought he'd chase me.

He didn't, of course, but that was all just theatre, to draw attention away from the house. The minute I was around the next corner and out of sight, I slowed. Then I made my way down the side of Meg's block and turned into the alley. As I rode along it to Meg's house, I looked toward the street. I couldn't see the van through the leaves, which meant nobody in the van could see me.

It turned out the house itself hid the back gate from the van, so even if the weeds hadn't been close to my height, I would have been hidden as I leaned my bike up against the fence.

I hesitated just a second. The forbidding forest of weeds in Meg's backyard looked anything but welcoming, even though a decaying boardwalk led through it to her back porch. But then I thought of Lorenzo, pleading for help.

I lifted the latch.

CHAPTER 4
I ENJOY SOME GIRL TALK

eg's backyard had obviously contained a dog at some point—just inside the gate and off to my right, an old doghouse crouched in the weeds like a witch's cottage in an enchanted forest—but, fortunately, was canine-free at the moment. I could see from the pattern of the weeds that there had once been a garden, too, but except for some rhubarb gone wild and a string of scraggly raspberry bushes, nothing edible grew there now.

The boardwalk led to the back porch, home to a greasy black barbecue and a couple of folding lawn chairs, the ancient kind with aluminum tubing and brightly coloured nylon webbing, now dirty and frayed. I picked my way gingerly through the weeds, stepping over the broken slats in the boardwalk, and finally climbed onto the deck. It sagged under my weight.

This would be easier if I'd ever said two words to her before, I thought, but easy or not, I had to talk to her. She was my only hope of figuring out what had happened to Lorenzo.

Of course, first I'd have to convince Meg that Lorenzo really had turned into . . . whatever he'd turned into.

A fireboy, I thought. It seemed as good a description as any.

I raised my hand to knock and then almost jumped out of my skin as a voice said, "What do you want?" behind me.

I spun. It was Meg, of course. Taller than me by two or three inches and skinnier, too, she wore faded blue jeans, a black T-shirt with the words DEAD PIRATES in white curving over a picture of a skull, and red sneakers. Startlingly green eyes peered at me suspiciously from beneath a tangled mop of red-blonde hair.

"Uh," I said. "Hi." Not the most scintillatingly brilliant start to our conversation, but she'd startled me.

She didn't say anything, just folded her arms across her chest, making her glare even more intimidating.

"I need to talk to you?" I added and winced, because I'd just up-talked, and I hate that? You know?

She didn't uncross her arms or soften her glare. "Why?"

"About what happened." This time, I managed to keep from adding a question mark. Barely. "On the bus trip."

Another long glare. "Why now?"

"Because . . ." My voice trailed off. This would take some working up to. "Because I . . . heard something . . . about... that."

No response.

"Please?" *That's supposed to be the magic word . . .*

Maybe it was. She considered me for another minute, then finally unfolded her arms. "Okay. But not here. There's a TV van out front. That's why I came in the back gate."

"I know," I said. "That's why I did, too. Why did they come today?"

"Because they're buzzards," Meg said. Her mouth tightened. "And it's the three-month anniversary. Come on." She led me back through the weedy backyard into the alley, where she stopped. "Do you have any money?"

I blinked. "Um . . . a little. Why?"

"Because I'm hungry," Meg said. "If I'm going to talk to you, the least you can do is buy me something to eat."

"Fair enough. Burger?"

"Hot dog."

"The Dog Pound?"

She grinned. She suddenly looked much less scary. "You read my mind."

"Do you have a bike?"

"Yeah." She took a few steps and pulled an old three-speed out from behind a bush—I'd walked right by it and never seen it.

"I'll get mine."

A few seconds later, we were rolling through the streets of Limberpine, having carefully avoided the one in front of Meg's house, where I hoped the TV van would sit all day, getting hotter and hotter.

Despite Limberpine being in the foothills of the Rockies, most of the town is pretty flat, except out on the edges, like where Dad and I live. And as I've already mentioned, it's also not very big. Cycling can get you anywhere pretty much as fast as a car—especially if you know all the shortcuts through alleys and empty lots and parks, and every kid in town does.

Fifteen minutes after we had climbed on our bikes, they were leaning up against the brick wall of The Dog Pound, located in an old building that used to be the town jail, and we had a hot dog apiece. I'd gone for my fave, a Texas Taco Dog (cheddar, nacho cheese, crumbled tortilla chips, onions, olives, sour cream, and guacamole). Meg had chosen a Mad Mac-n-Cheese Dog (a hot dog topped with macaroni-and-cheese—it looked awful to me, but as long as it made her happy and she'd talk to me, I was willing to live and let gag).

I bought an order of fries for us to share and a Coke apiece, and then we went outside to sit at one of the picnic tables arranged in front of the old jail. (There were tables inside, too, but nobody ever sat there when the weather was good.) I watched in admiration as Meg practically inhaled her food. I wondered if she'd ever entered the hot-dog eating contest at the fair—she'd make a killing.

She finished her dog before I'd taken three bites of my own and then gave the remainder of the fries a longing look. I'd only had a couple myself, but I shoved the rest over to her, and she snatched a handful. "Sorry," she mumbled from a full mouth as she shovelled them in. "Not a lot of food around our house. Mom's . . . out."

I remembered hearing Meg didn't have a dad. I didn't remember why. Maybe I'd ask sometime, but I didn't think two hot dogs and a few fries had brought us to quite the necessary level of BFF-ness yet. So, instead, I said, "I've been wanting to talk to you ever since it happened." Not true; I hadn't even *thought* of talking to her until hunka-hunka-burning Lorenzo showed up in my back yard. Though now I wondered why. Meg was the only one who had come back from the class trip—the last person to see all my friends (I refused to add the word "alive" to the end of that thought). Why *hadn't* I wanted to talk to her?

Maybe I was afraid she'd tell me she thought everyone else was dead. Maybe I didn't want to think about it. I don't know. Sometimes, my own brain confuses me.

But here I was now, and here she was, and Lorenzo

was . . . somewhere. Definitely not dead. Just . . . different. And at least some of the other kids were wherever he was, too. Hopefully, all of them.

"Yeah?" Meg said. She took another fry. She'd slowed down a little about halfway through them, but she clearly wasn't done yet. "Then why didn't you?"

Since I'd just asked myself the same thing and hadn't found an answer, all I could say was, "I don't know. But something happened last night that . . . made me make the effort."

"Yeah?" Meg said again. She ate the fry. "What?" She took another one.

I hesitated. Did I tell her the truth?

Not yet. She'd run away screaming. Or just laugh at me. I didn't want either one.

"A dream," I said. Not exactly a lie. I'd *thought* it was a dream at first. "Of Lorenzo. I miss him. I miss all of them."

"I don't," Meg said. I stared at her, shocked. "I *don't*," she insisted. "I only came to the school halfway through April. I barely talked to any of you, and hardly any of you talked to me."

"I'm sorry . . ."

She waved her half-eaten fry at me. "No, you're not. And I'm not mad at you. It's just the way it is. I've been in a lot of schools. It's always the same. Everyone already has friends, sometimes kids they've been in school with since kindergarten. It takes time to make new friends, and since I'm usually not around very long, I don't try. And since I don't try, nobody tries to make friends with me, either." She swallowed the rest of the fry, wiped her fingers on her napkin, and reached for her Coke. "I figured we'd move over the summer, and I'd never see anyone from Limberpine ever again."

"But you're still here." It came out a little sharper than I intended.

Meg took a big swig of Coke and set down the red plastic glass. "Yeah," she said. "Mom actually *likes* her job this time. She's not drinking . . . as much. Maybe she won't get fired."

"Oh." The conversation was veering into territory I didn't want to explore. "Well, then, as the only survivors of Dr. Ballard's Grade 7 science class, we should stick together."

"Should we?" Meg swiped her napkin across her mouth, leaned back in her chair, and folded her arms. "Thanks for the food. Now, what do you *really* want?"

I looked down at my hands, wrapped around my own red plastic tumbler, the condensation on its pebbled sides cold under my fingers. "In my . . . dream . . . Lorenzo told me I should talk to you."

"So? I had a dream where I jumped off a building and flew. I'm not going to climb up onto the top of the gym and try it in real life."

"This dream was different. It seemed . . . real." Although thinking about it again on a sunny morning outside The Dog Pound, I almost doubted what I'd seen myself. Maybe it *had* been a dream. Maybe I hadn't really run out into the night to talk to a pillar of flame . . .

No. I remember how cold my bare feet had been in the wet grass and leaves. I remembered stripping off my wet pyjamas. I remembered Dad swearing when he tripped over them. I remembered the cold smack of them in my face. There was no doubt I'd gone outside in the middle of the night. And I'd never been a sleepwalker.

Meg studied me for another long moment, eyes narrowed. Finally, she sighed, unfolded her arms, and leaned forward for the third-last fry. I helped myself to the second-last one, hoping she'd let me have the last one, too: I was feeling seriously short-changed, fry-wise. As I dipped mine in the puddle of ketchup she'd poured into one corner of the cardboard basket, she leaned back, popped hers into her mouth, chewed it, swallowed it, and finally said, "All right. I'll tell you what I saw. Maybe it was a dream, too. I don't know. All I know is . . . it was weird."

As weird as a boy made out of fire? "Go on," I said, and took a ketchupy bite of my own fried-potato stick.

"It wasn't an accident," she said.

I blinked. "But I saw the photos—"

She shook her head impatiently. "That's not what I mean. Yes, we crashed, but not by accident." She took a deep breath. "We were *thrown* off the road."

"Thrown? I don't—"

"By a monster." Meg's eyes searched my face like she was daring me to laugh. I didn't. "A *thing* made out of dirt. It rose up right beside the road and gave us a shove as we went around that corner. Not everyone saw it, but everyone screamed as we tipped over. The bus should have crashed into the trees. Probably would have killed us all if that had happened—but two more . . . *things* . . . caught us."

I realized my mouth was hanging open. I closed it and leaned forward. "Were they made of fire?"

She blinked. "Fire? What? No. They were made of water. Shaped like women. They cushioned the fall."

"And then what happened?"

"I don't know." Meg picked up the final French fry and stabbed it into the puddle of ketchup like she was driving a knife into an already bloody wound. "I passed out."

I sighed. I'd really wanted that last fry. "Did you hit your head?"

"No," Meg said. "All the camping equipment crashed down on me—sleeping bags and backpacks and crap like that, all this stuff that was behind me and in the seat next to me because I was sitting in the very back, as far away from the others as I could get—but nothing hit me that hard. I was starting to push my way out when I just . . . fainted, I guess." She shoved the fry into her mouth angrily. "When I woke up, the cops were there, and everyone else except Dr. Ballard had vanished."

"Did he tell the cops about the . . . things?"

"No," Meg said. "He said he passed out before the crash, so he wouldn't have seen them. He thought that was *why* we'd crashed. They sent him off for a medical examination, but as far as I know, they didn't find anything wrong with him."

"Have you seen him since it happened?"

"No," Meg said. "And I don't want to."

I looked away from her, across the street to the town's only gas station, the same gas station the bus had refuelled at before it headed up the mountain. It was the last place anyone other than Meg and Dr. Ballard had seen Lorenzo and the rest of the class before the accident. "Did *you* tell the police what you saw?"

Meg snorted. "Do I *look* stupid? They'd either decide I'm crazy or I was high on drugs. Probably find a way to blame me for causing the crash. Then they'd start talking to Mom, and if they did that . . ." She stopped, shaking her head. "No. You're the only one I've told the truth." She looked down. "And now you probably think I'm crazy or was high, too."

"No," I said. "No, I don't."

Her head came up. She looked surprised. "You don't?"

I shook my head, mind made up. "No. And here's why." I took a deep breath and then told her my story.

Her eyes widened as I spoke, but she didn't interrupt. When I finished, she said, "That's why you asked if the things I saw were made of fire."

I nodded.

"Dirt . . . air . . . fire . . ." Meg said. "Why does that seem familiar?"

"There's an old rock band called Earth, Wind & Fire," I offered. "One of Grandpa's favourites."

Meg snapped her fingers. "That's it."

"You've heard of them?" I said, surprised. "They're *ancient*."

She waved her hand impatiently. "I've never heard of the band. But I've heard of Earth, Wind, Fire, and Water. The four classical elements. Dr. Ballard told us about them."

"That's right!" I remembered, too: in fact, it hadn't been long before the fatal . . . *no*, I thought fiercely, *interrupted* . . . bus trip. We'd been talking about the periodic table, and he'd started by telling us about the four classical elements, the things people a long time ago thought made up everything. It had been interesting because he'd tied it into alchemists, about which I already knew a few things because of a) *Harry Potter and the Philosopher's Stone* and b) *Full Metal Alchemist Brotherhood*, my favourite anime. "Lorenzo has been turned into fire. You saw a man made of earth and women made of water. What if they were people, too, but were turned into those things by . . . someone?"

"You think that's what happened to your friends?"

"*Our* friends."

She shook her head stubbornly. "Yours."

"Fine. Our *classmates*, then. Yes, maybe. And that

means . . . they're not dead! At least Lorenzo isn't, and he thinks there are others wherever he is . . . his body is, I mean." I locked my eyes on hers. "We have to figure out where they are—and save them all!"

If this had been a movie, there would have been a dramatic swell of music at that point.

Instead, a pimply-faced high school boy in a red-and-white uniform with a panting cartoon dog on the left breast came outside and said, "You kids done?"

No, we're just beginning! I said dramatically in my head, trying to salvage the movie, but out loud, all I said was, "Yeah, thanks." The boy picked up our tumblers and carried them inside. We pushed our garbage into one of the nearby cans, to the annoyance of half a dozen flies.

"Right," Meg said. She licked a stray bit of leftover ketchup off her thumb. "Now what?"

"We need more information. We need to talk to Lorenzo."

"Right," Meg said again. "And how do we do that, exactly?"

I grinned at her. "How'd you like to come to my house for a sleepover?"

CHAPTER 5

I HAVE SOME FRIENDS OVER

"You think he'll show up?" Meg whispered.

Meg and I were staring out the window of my bedroom into the backyard, both of us dressed for bed: in her case, pyjama shorts and a long black T-shirt bearing the cryptic message AMERICAN TURTLE WORLD TOUR in silver block letters on the front and a list of cities (only one of which, Toronto, was outside the U.S.—some world tour) on the back; in my case, my spare pyjamas, one size too small, which meant my ankles, wrists, and belly button were all exposed. My usual pyjamas still lay in a damp lump on my floor, the housecleaning elves having let me down again.

We'd officially gone to bed an hour before and had turned off the light to prove it. Half an hour ago, I'd heard Dad walk along the creaky hallway floorboards to his room and the door close behind him. The house was silent, except for us.

"I hope so," I whispered back. But right then, there was nothing in the backyard but grass and weeds and nothing in the woods but trees and darkness.

Meg had instantly said "yes" to the invitation to a sleepover. "Shouldn't you ask your Mom?" I'd said, and "No," she'd said rather shortly, and that had been that. We'd ridden our bikes back to her house—where the TV van was still parked out front—and she'd gone in the back door to grab her stuff. She hadn't invited me in, so I'd sat on the sagging back porch, trying to make sense of what she'd told me and what I'd seen, and always coming back to what I'd told her: we needed more information. We needed to talk to Lorenzo.

I wanted Meg to see him so she'd know I hadn't made him up. And to be honest, I desperately wanted to see him again myself just to be sure I'd seen him the first time—which, oddly, would help convince me just a little more firmly that Meg hadn't made up what she'd told me, either.

I mean, I'd never have believed her if I hadn't seen Fire-Lorenzo first. Mobile man-shaped mounds of mud? Wandering water-women? She was right: the cops would have been sure she was either crazy or high, in which case she might be locked up in some juvenile detention and/or detox centre right now and not standing shoulder-to-shoulder with me, looking out through my open window.

At least it's not raining, I thought, staring down into the darkness. But the air coming in was cold all the same. It was still summer, but we were high enough, up here in the foothills, that on a clear night in late August, it wasn't at all impossible to get frost. I didn't think it was quite that cold out tonight, but it was a sure hint that winter was coming.

Another fifteen minutes went by. I yawned; I couldn't help it.

Meg punched my arm. "None of tha—aat," she said, caught in the middle of the last word by a yawn of her own. "It's contagious."

Another yawn welled up, but I pressed my lips together and more-or-less contained it.

Fifteen more minutes. *At least Dad is sure to be asleep by now*, I thought. We'd started out standing; now we were both kneeling, resting our heads on our arms, looking out into the night. *So, if . . . when . . . Lorenzo shows up . . .*

I didn't finish that thought. Sometime later, I jerked out of the doze I'd slipped into without meaning to as Meg hissed, "Sam!"

I lifted my head.

Fire flickered among the trees behind the barn.

"Is it him?" Meg whispered.

"What else could it be?" I whispered back. But I hesitated. What if it wasn't? What if it was some other fire . . . person? What if whoever was doing whatever it was he was doing to Lorenzo had done it to someone else, too, and *that* was who was flickering among the trees?

That barely made sense, I thought. I straightened. "Okay," I murmured. "Follow my footsteps through the hall and down the stairs. I know where to step to make the floor creak as little as possible."

"As little as possible" wasn't the same as not creaking at *all*, and I kept stopping, hand trailing along the wall, holding my breath, while I listened for the sound of Dad getting out of bed. He would *not* be happy with us if that happened, although he'd been happy enough to welcome Meg—I think he thought it was about time I made a new friend since all my other friends had mysteriously vanished.

Why not *wake him up? Show him Lorenzo, if that's who's out there?* a part of my brain whispered. *He could help. We'd be careful. We wouldn't—*

But Lorenzo had seemed terrified by the suggestion, and I

had a horrible feeling he was right. If I told Dad . . . *if* he believed me . . . he'd take charge. He'd go barreling around, demanding the authorities start a search, demanding answers from the school—and if Lorenzo was right, whoever had turned him into the human torch would kill him and all the rest of my friends . . .

. . . and it would be my fault.

We have to do this by ourselves. Meg and me. No one else.

We reached the bottom of the stairs. The ground floor didn't creak as much, so we could move faster, although we still had to be careful to open the back door as noiselessly as possible. Two seconds later, we were running across the backyard in our bare feet. For a horrible minute, I couldn't see any light among the trees, and I thought Lorenzo had left already, but then we reached the far end of the barn, and there he was, farther back in the forest than last time, standing among some rocks that poked out of the ground a few feet up the hillside.

Meg stopped dead. "No way," she breathed.

I glared at her. "You didn't believe me?"

"I *thought* I did, but . . . wow."

"Come on," I said impatiently and hurried to where Lorenzo waited. The old leaves and pine needles and twigs scattered across the forest floor were wet and cold, and the air nipped at my exposed midriff, and I wished we'd taken time to put on shoes and maybe bathrobes. But I forgot about my chilly toes and goosebumps as we reached Lorenzo.

Both his face and body were better defined tonight, as though he were somehow even *more* completely made out of fire. The heat coming off of him was more than welcome in the chill air. "Sam!" he cried. Then his burning eyes flicked over my shoulder. "Meg?"

"She saw what happened," I panted, leaning over, hands on knees, while I caught my breath. "When the bus crashed."

Lorenzo moved closer. Meg took a step back, her eyes wide, the whites tinged red by the light of his burning body. Lorenzo stopped. "Tell me what you saw!" he said—commanded, really. His voice hissed and crackled.

Meg licked her lips. "We were attacked. By . . . things."

"Things like me?"

"No," Meg said. "Different. There was a big one made of dirt—mud, really—and two more made of water. They looked like women. The dirt thing threw us off the road, and the water-women caught us."

"And then?" Lorenzo's gaze suddenly jerked off to the right as though he'd heard something; he stared that way for a second, then looked at Meg again, with *literally* burning intensity. "And then?"

"I don't know," she said. "I passed out. I don't know why. When I woke up, I was buried in the camping equipment, and the rest of you were gone. The cops pulled me out."

"What about Dr. Ballard?" Lorenzo looked at me. "You said they found him, too."

I nodded, but Meg answered. "He was still unconscious. I saw the ambulance guys trying to rouse him. He woke up while they were examining me. He said he didn't remember anything."

"Did you ask him if he saw what you saw?"

"I didn't have a chance," Meg said. "But I gave him a significant look."

I blinked. "A what?"

She shrugged. "You know, wriggled my eyebrows. Jerked my head toward the wreck. But he didn't react. Except to frown like he thought I was crazy. I wasn't going to come right out and *tell* him what I saw because then I was *sure* he'd think I was crazy. I figured if *he'd* seen something he would have told the cops for sure. They'd have believed the science teacher."

I looked back at Lorenzo. "We're going to find you," I said. I drew on all my acting skills (I'd played the Dormouse in our school's riveting production of *Alice in Wonderland* in Grade 6; admittedly, it had consisted mostly of sleeping, but I'd done it *very* convincingly) to make it sound like I believed it. "But we need more information. Isn't there *anything* else you can tell us?"

Lorenzo's head suddenly snapped left. "Do you hear that?"

I stared into the darkness. I couldn't hear anything. There wasn't even a breath of wind to stir the trees, and the hollow in which our house nestled cut off the sound of traffic from the town—not that there would be much traffic this time of night. Nothing was open except maybe the Bitterroot Bar, and it was clear on the other side of Limberpine. "I don't hear anything."

Lorenzo stared into the woods for another long moment, then turned back to us. "I told you, I'm in what looks like a dorm room in a really lousy school. No windows. Really ugly mud-coloured carpet. Puke-green walls—plaster over concrete, I think. Old-fashioned light fixture, one of those upside-down-wok things. When the man or the nurse opens the door, all I can see is a hallway with an even uglier carpet and what looks like a bulletin board on the wall."

"What about sounds? Or smells?"

"It just smells like damp carpet and mildew," Lorenzo said. "Like an old building that nobody's using anymore.

Sounds . . ." He shook his head. "Doors banging. And some-times, off in the distance, shouts or . . . or crying."

"The other kids?" Meg said. "He's got the whole class?"

"Except for you." Lorenzo suddenly burned brighter. "What makes you special?"

Meg's eyes narrowed. "Pretty sure I'd be a prisoner right about now, too, if I hadn't been buried under you rich kids' fancy camping equipment. And don't you think you should be a little nicer to someone who's going to try to rescue you?"

Lorenzo's flames dimmed again, and he ducked his burning head. "Sorry," he said. "Sorry. It's just . . . I want out of here. I *have* to get out of here. We all do. I can't . . ." His head jerked up. "Look out!"

I jerked around, sensed something swinging toward me, and ducked, falling backward, cold water promptly soaking my butt through my pyjamas. Then Lorenzo swept past me, so close I gasped from the sudden heat, and slammed into the thing that had attacked me.

It was shaped like a man, but it was bigger than any man I'd ever seen, at least eight feet tall, maybe ten. It was made of mud, thick and black and oozing. Its face was just a blob with two black openings for eyes. It made no sound as Lorenzo's blazing body slammed into its slimy one, but it staggered back as a cloud of steam exploded from it. Sticky black clots of slime splattered me.

Meg had kept her feet; she grabbed my arm and hauled me upright. "Get away from it!" she cried. "That's the thing that attacked the bus!"

We scrambled into the woods and then turned to watch Lorenzo grappling with the mud-man. It towered over Loren-zo's slim, fiery form, but Lorenzo was fast, dashing around it like a small dog attacking a big one, and every time he hit the thing, another burst of steam ripped chunks from it. It swung massive fists at Lorenzo but missed every time, and all the time, it was losing form and mass . . .

. . . and then, just like that, it collapsed into nothing more than a pile of muck.

Lorenzo swung around, fire blazing hotter than ever. "Sam? Meg? Are you all right?"

We exchanged glances. We were both splattered with mud from head to toe. "You okay?" I asked Meg.

She nodded.

We walked back toward Lorenzo. The heat from him felt comforting.

I stared at the mud pile. "Is it gone for good?"

"I don't think it works like that," Lorenzo said. "I mean, when I lose this form, I find myself back in my own body." He looked down at the heap of muck. "This guy might be the same."

"Or maybe he doesn't have a body anymore," Meg said, contributing her usual dose of cheeriness to the conversation. "Maybe you killed him."

"Killed . . .?" Lorenzo's flaming face looked stricken. "I don't want to kill anyone!" Then, his expression contracted into a fiery frown. "Except maybe the man who's doing this."

"But what is he?" I looked at Lorenzo. Fighting the mud-man had somehow brought him into even sharper focus: now he was so solidly formed he looked like a Greek statue made of fire rather than the vaguely boy-shaped bonfire he'd seemed the night before. "What are you . . . becoming?"

"Earth. Water. Air. Fire," Meg said. "Remember?"

Lorenzo's fiery eyes widened. "The four classical elements!" He'd been in the same class we had when we'd learned about them, but he'd probably known about them already—he read a lot. Even more than me, and that's saying something. "I'm Fire. This guy was Earth. You said you saw two 'water-women.'"

"That leaves Air," Meg said.

"So, this mysterious tormentor of yours is turning people into . . . the four classical elements?" I said.

"Into *elementals*," Lorenzo said excitedly. "That's the word. Elementals. I've fought them."

I blinked. "What?"

"In computer games. And in *Dungeons and Dragons*." Then, his eyes widened further. "Oh! And that explains the name I heard the nurse—"

His crackling voice cut off as something else came rushing through the trees, downhill, smashing into the outcropping of rock where Lorenzo had first appeared with so much force the massive boulders shifted: as tall as the mud-man but made of water and female in form. Lorenzo spun to face it . . . her. "Run!" he shouted and dashed up the hill.

Believe me, I wanted to—but I didn't. I had to see what happened to him. We backed away, but not far, pressing our backs against two tree trunks, watching as Lorenzo crashed into the water-woman.

Again, steam exploded and went on and on, gouts of it shooting out from the . . . elemental? . . . but not diminishing her the way it had the mud-man. The steam just swirled around, then leaped back to rejoin the water-woman's glistening form, which engulfed Lorenzo's bright, burning body . . .

. . . which started to dim.

Enveloped by water and steam, glowing no more brightly than the last dying ember in a fireplace, he managed to scream one last word, a strange word, one I'd never heard before.

And then he . . . went out.

The water-woman vanished an instant later, collapsing, water foaming white over the steaming rocks for a few seconds before the already-damp forest floor swallowed it up.

And then, of course, the light came on in our backyard, and I heard my Dad calling, "Meg? Sam?"

"Coming!" I shouted because I didn't want him worrying, but to Meg, I said, *sotto voce*, "We are in *so* much trouble."

"Not as much as Lorenzo," she said, and I couldn't argue with that.

Covered in mud, feet freezing, yet another set of pyjamas ruined, I led her back toward our house to face the music.

CHAPTER 6
I PRACTICE MY GOOGLE-FU

Dad ushered us into the kitchen. We stood there, shivering, while he glared at us, his gaze travelling from our bare feet up our mud-spattered clothes to our pale faces (at least, Meg's was pale, so I figured mine was, too). Meg looked at the linoleum. I looked at Dad, waiting for the hammer to fall.

"Sam," Dad finally said, and I could tell that he was only not yelling because Meg was standing next to me, "I told you the last time . . . which should have been the last time . . . how dangerous it is to sneak out at night. What were you doing out there?"

Meg looked up. "It's my fault, Mr. MacReady," she said, surprising me. "I wanted to see the barn."

"In the middle of the night?" Dad said. "Barefoot? In your nightclothes?"

"It . . . seemed like a good idea at the time?" Meg said. For once, I approved of up-talking. It made her sound innocent. (Or slightly stupid, but either could work in our favour.)

Dad looked from her to me. I could tell he didn't believe

her. "Is that true, Sam?" he said, and I shivered again, more from the tone of his voice than from the cold water and mud soaking my pyjamas. I didn't want to lie to him, but I couldn't tell him the truth.

I settled for shrugging.

Dad kept looking at me. "And how did you get covered in mud?"

"We fell," Meg said brightly. "It's slippery."

Dad still didn't look at her. I really, really wished he would because his gaze was making *me* very uncomfortable. "All right," he said at last after an uncomfortable silence. "Go upstairs and get out of your wet clothes. Sam, do you have something else for Meg to sleep in?"

I nodded. I had an oversized T-shirt she could wear as a nightgown, although she might not appreciate the fact it was decorated with adorable white kittens with pink bows around their necks instead of the name of an obscure rock band.

"Then get to bed, both of you. I don't want to hear another peep."

"Yes, Daddy."

"Yes, Mr. MacReady."

I didn't look at Meg as we climbed up to my room, leaving damp, bare footprints on the stairs. Inside my room, I handed Meg the T-shirt—she raised her eyebrows at the kittens but didn't say anything—and grabbed an old night-gown from the dresser. We got out of our wet things and into the dry ones, which felt good.

I'd put a sleeping bag on the floor for Meg, but I gestured to her to climb into bed with me, both to warm up and so we could talk.

We lay with our heads almost touching. "Your Dad's pretty mad," Meg whispered.

"I don't blame him," I whispered back. "Good thing you were with me. Thanks for speaking up first."

I felt her shrug. "I figured he wouldn't yell at me the way he would at you."

"The yelling is probably still coming." I sighed. Dad never *used* to yell at me, but since Mom had died, his temper had gotten shorter. But like I'd just told Meg, I didn't blame him. I'd have yelled, too, if I were a parent and my kid had sneaked out twice in two nights and come back wet and cold both times.

And if my kid told me she'd seen a flaming friend and been attacked by a mud-man and water-woman, and that was why she was wet and cold, I'd take her to see a doctor. So, although I empathized with Dad, I still wasn't going to tell him the truth. Not just to protect myself, but to protect Lorenzo.

"What did Lorenzo shout just before he disappeared?" Meg whispered then.

That was the big question, wasn't it? "I don't know," I murmured back. "I heard something like 'pair of chelses.' But what's a 'chelse'? And why do they come in pairs?"

We were both silent for a second.

"How do we find out what it means?" Meg finally whispered.

"Google, I guess," I said. My eyes were closing. "In the morning."

"In the morning."

A MINUTE LATER, it seemed like that's what it was.

Meg had moved back to her sleeping bag at some point, so I had the bed to myself. I blinked up at the ceiling. Dad hadn't come in to wake us up, and the house was quiet. He must have already gone off to his new job. If there was going to be any yelling, it would wait until supper.

Maybe by then, he'll have forgotten about it. Or maybe now that he has that job, he won't be yelling as much.

It was a nice thought, but it was followed by a much less nice thought: Lorenzo. What had he said to us? A clue, to look for a "pair of chelses," as I had heard it? Or something else?

"Meg?" I said. "Are you awake?"

"Nggh."

I took that as a yes. "We need to get up. We need to figure out what to do."

"Nggh." A heavy breath. "All right." She yawned. "I'm awake. Kind of."

Ten minutes later, we were dressed and downstairs, with a bowl of cereal and a glass of orange juice apiece, trying to figure out what Lorenzo had said just before he disappeared and not having much success. I'd said we should Google it, and after going around in circles a few more times, that's what we tried to do, adjourning to the family computer, which was set up on its own desk in the living room (Dad was determined that if I wanted to use a computer, I'd use it where he could see me, ignoring the fact I was home alone half the time).

"Pair of chelses" turned into "pair of Chelseas" which got us a bunch of pictures of stylish boots—hard to believe that was what Lorenzo had been going for, although I wouldn't have minded a pair of Chelseas, after I got a look at them.

Next, I tried "pairachelses" as all one word or a name and

got nothing. Same with "pairofchelses," "pairajelses," "pairofjelses" and "pair a jelses."

"Maybe it's not 'pair a' or 'pair of,'" Meg said. "Maybe it's 'para.' You know, like 'paranormal' or 'parachute.' "

"Good thought," I said and changed my search to "parachelses." This brought me the suggestion of "parachesis," which was exciting until I read the definition: *A figure of speech where the same sound is repeated in words that are in close succession.* The example, *Peter Piper picked a prodigious peck of pickled peppers, polished persimmons, and preposterously pilgarlic pumpkins,* distracted me with the previously unknown word "pilgarlic," defined as *a man looked upon with humorous contempt or mock pity,* though what that had to do with pumpkins eluded me. But I didn't seem to be any closer to figuring out what Lorenzo had been trying to communicate.

"Try spelling 'chelses' different," said Meg, peering over my shoulder.

So I tried "parachelsis." *Showing results for Paracelsus,* Google said, offering a spelling I never would have thought of on my own.

As usual, the first entry was from *Wikipedia.* I read it out loud."Paracelsus; late 1493–September 24, 1541), born Philippus Aureolus Theophrastus Bombastus von Hohenheim, was a Swiss German philosopher, physician, botanist, astrologer, and general occultist." I stopped, eyes wide. "Hohenheim!"

Meg looked at me. "Gesundheit?"

"Hohenheim!" I pointed at the screen. "He's a character in *Full Metal Alchemist Brotherhood.*"

"Oh . . . kay?"

"It's an anime."

"A Japanese cartoon?" Meg said doubtfully.

"They're not just cartoons, they're . . ." I bit off my retort. Much as I enjoyed explaining/discussing/complaining about anime—Lorenzo and I used to talk about it for hours—this probably wasn't the time. "Never mind. The point is, he's an alchemist."

"Dr. Ballard talked about them," Meg said. "Old-fashioned chemists, right?"

"Kind of. And one of the things alchemists focused on was transformation—changing one thing into another."

"Like turning a living boy into a fireboy!" Meg said with sudden excitement. "Paracelsus! That's got to be what Lorenzo yelled!"

I stared at the screen. "But what can Paracelsus possibly have to do with whatever is going on here? He's been dead for centuries!"

"Did this Paracelsus dude have anything to say about Earth, Wind & Fire or other old rock bands?"

I laughed. "Let's see." I typed in "elements" and "Paracelsus. " The first hit was the *Wikipedia* entry on Paracelsus I'd already seen. But the second link led to an article called "The Elements and Their Inhabitants," and as soon as I started reading it, I knew I'd hit the jackpot. "Wow, oh wow," I said. "This calls Paracelsus the 'prince of alchemists' and 'true possessor of the Philosopher's Stone!'"

"The Philosopher's Stone?" Meg blinked. "Like in *Harry Potter*?"

"The same!" I said excitedly. "And remember, one of the things the Philosopher's Stone is supposed to be able to do is to grant immortality. If this Paracelsus *really* had it, he could still be alive."

"And more than five hundred years old?" Meg shook her head violently. "That's impossible."

"Says the girl who's seen two mud-men, three water-women, and a boy made out of fire?"

Meg blinked again. "Um . . . point taken."

I leaned closer to the screen to read the entry. "Paracelsus believed that 'just as visible Nature is populated by an infinite number of living creatures,' so the 'tenuous principles of the visible elements are inhabited by a host of peculiar beings' called 'elementals: living entities, many resembling human beings in shape.' "

We looked at each other. "Like the things that attacked the bus!" Meg said.

"And like Lorenzo," I said.

"So, you think this undead Paracelsus dude is turning kids into elementals?"

"I don't know. Maybe." I read on. It was tough going: the author clearly hadn't been focused on writing at a Grade 8 level. But I picked up a few things, passing along the important tidbits to Meg."Paracelsus thought there were two kinds of flesh, the first 'that which we have all inherited through Adam, the visible, corporeal flesh,' and the second something he called 'transubstantial flesh,' which did *not* descend from Adam and 'was not subject to the limitations of the former.' Elementals are made of this 'transubstantial flesh.'"

I frowned at the screen. "But it sounds like he believed there were elements of both kinds of flesh in human beings. So, if he could pull the transubstantial flesh out of the substantial flesh, maybe he could turn it into one of these elementals . . .?" I read on. " 'They are beings occupying a place between men and spirits, resembling men and spirits, resembling men and women in their organization and form, and resembling spirits in the rapidity of their locomotion.' " I stared at Meg. "Which is why Lorenzo can flit from place to place so fast! It all makes perfect sense."

Meg snorted. "I'm glad you think so. I didn't understand half of what you just said."

I pointed at the article. "According to Paracelsus, a water elemental is called a nymph, an air elemental is called a sylph, an earth elemental is a gnome, and a fire elemental is a salamander."

"So, Lorenzo is a *salamander*?"

"I guess so." Despite everything, I grinned. "He's going to *love* that. He had a pet salamander for a while."

"What happened to it?"

"Nothing good. It got out, and weeks later, they found it mummified behind the refrigerator."

"Eww, gross." Meg made a face, then peered at the screen again. "Does it say how you turn an elemental back into a human being?"

"No," I said, "because it doesn't say anything about turning a human being into an elemental to begin with." I scrolled through the article. "Thing is, there were all sorts of opinions about elementals, and they all contradicted each other. Even some of the stuff Paracelsus said about them contradicts what Lorenzo seems to be."

"If Paracelsus is still alive," Meg said, "he's had a very long time to study up on the topic. Maybe he's figured out some stuff he didn't figure out in his first lifetime. You could probably learn a lot over five centuries!"

I clicked Print, and as the printer whirred to life and started spitting out paper—the article was a dozen pages long —I leaned back in the chair. "If Paracelsus is alive, how do we find him? And how do we stop a centuries-old sorcerer?"

"It would help if we knew what he looked like," Meg said. "Are there any drawings or paintings of this guy?"

I turned back to the computer. "Lots," I said after a minute. "They don't look very much alike, though."

Meg looked over my shoulder. "Most of them show him as pretty bald. And they seem to agree he had a big nose."

"But some of them show him fat, some show him skinny, and he's not even bald or big-nosed in *all* of them," I pointed out.

"They all agree he didn't smile much," Meg said.

I sighed. "So, we're looking for a frowning man who may or may not have a big nose, who may or may not be bald, may or may not be tall, and may or may not be fat."

"Not much help," Meg admitted.

"We need to talk to Lorenzo some more. Maybe he'll come back tonight. Can you stay over again?"

Meg shrugged. "Sure. I'll just leave Mom a voice message. But will your Dad let me after last night?"

"Yes," I said, though I wasn't as certain about that as I tried to make myself sound. "But we for *sure* have to not get caught if we go out to see Lorenzo again." I pointed at the sunshine streaming in through the windows. "At least it's sunny. Drying up. No reason we should get wet and muddy."

Meg looked outside. "It's still morning. What do we do today?"

I'd already been thinking about that, and I had my answer ready. "The spot where you ran off the road isn't that far out of town, is it?"

"Maybe ten miles."

"Feel up to a bike ride?"

CHAPTER 7
I VISIT THE SCENE OF THE CRIME

Ten miles isn't a terrifically long bike ride on flat ground. Trouble was, the curve where the accident had happened was ten miles up the mountain road that led to the campground the class never reached. I regretted my suggestion (and was wondering if a thirteen-year-old girl could have a heart attack) before we'd gone two miles. A couple of stretches were so steep we had to get off our bikes and push them up the hill. I just kept reminding myself that when we headed home, it would all be downhill, and concentrated on breathing.

Okay, puffing.

Noon had come and gone by the time we reached the spot. We leaned our bikes up against some trees, pulled out the water bottles we'd packed, and sucked on them as we walked over to the bend in the road the bus had failed to negotiate. "Here," Meg said, pointing to the ground on the inside of the curve. "Here's where I saw the mud thing. It just heaved up out of the ground and gave the bus a shove."

I squatted and stared at the ground. It looked like any

other ground . . . or did it? Were there fewer pine needles on that patch than in most places? There certainly weren't any bushes or other undergrowth—which was just what you'd expect if a mud-man had crawled out of the ground at that point.

At least, I *guessed* that's what you'd expect. Mud-men crawling out of the ground wasn't anything I'd had any reason to expect until then. Any more than my best friend turning into the Human Torch.

I straightened up. "And then what happened?"

Meg looked both ways, then crossed the road. On the other side, just at the edge of the trees, deep gouges scarred the earth. "Here's where we ended up. We landed here." She pointed at the ground. "Then we slid over there." She pointed toward the trees.

"And the . . . water-women?" I remembered what that article I'd found online had called water elementals. "The nymphs, I guess?" *Nymphs* was an okay word, but there was no way I was going to call mud-men strong enough to over-turn a moving bus *gnomes*. Gnomes were lawn ornaments.

Meg led me to the end of the skid marks and stopped. "They were right here, at the edge of the woods. If they hadn't been, we'd have smashed into the trees, and I wouldn't be here talking to you."

I didn't see any weird marks where Meg said the nymphs had appeared, but any traces of water would have long since vanished. I could see what Meg meant, though: if the bus had slammed into those trees . . . there wouldn't have been much left of it.

Or anyone on board it.

The thought gave me a funny feeling. I didn't like it.

I'd hoped seeing where the accident (*Except it wasn't an*

accident, was it? It was an attack!) had happened might result in a blinding flash of inspiration, revealing to me what we should do next, how we could find Lorenzo and the others. But I didn't feel particularly inspired. Or blinded.

"They brought in dogs to see if they could track the kids, didn't they?" I said, looking around. Rocks and trees and trees and rocks. Lots of both. Every last one of them had been there when whatever happened happened, but they weren't talking.

Stupid rocks and trees.

"Yeah," Meg said. "Couldn't find a trail."

"They must have been carried away," I said. "Maybe by one of the things you saw. Mud-men or water-women . .. nymphs . . . wouldn't leave a scent."

"That's what I figure."

"Lucky you were buried in sleeping bags. But why did they leave Dr. Ballard behind?"

"Too old, maybe? They clearly wanted kids."

I chewed on my lip. "How long before help showed up?"

"Three or four hours."

"Nobody else came along in all that time?" I looked at the road. The campground up at the top of the mountain was popular not only with campers but also with tourists because it offered a scenic overview of the valley.

"I was unconscious," Meg pointed out. "But what I heard was that a fallen tree had blocked the road. Someone trying to get up to the campground called it in. Emergency crews came to clear it away and then came on up the road to make sure no other trees were down—they figured there must have been a freak storm or something. That's when they found the bus."

"A tree down," I said. "Bet an elemental did that, too." This whole thing had been planned, presumably—if our garbled hearing of what Lorenz said hadn't sent us on a wild goose chase—by this Paracelsus dude. Somehow, he had known the class was going to be heading up the mountain.

Which meant he had spies in the town. Maybe in the school itself.

And suddenly, I *did* have a blinding flash of inspiration.

The vice-principal!

Johan Reiniger was his name. A German name, like Hohenheim, Paracelsus's real name. He'd only been at the school for a year, brought in after the previous vice-principal, Mr. Donovan, resigned suddenly. (Nobody told the kids why, but we all knew it was because he showed up drunk at a school board meeting and yelled at the superintendent for giving him a bad performance review. News like that tends to get around a small town.)

Vice-Principal Reiniger was tall, thin, blond-haired, and blue-eyed and had a noticeable accent, though not a very thick one. He got called a Nazi behind his back, not only because of the German thing, but because he was, to put it mildly, strict—as in an hour of detention for forgetting to take off your shoes before entering the gym strict. As in cancelling a basketball trip to Edmonton because one of the team members cheated on a test strict. That kind of thing.

Totally Nazi.

It all fit. "Reiniger," I said to Meg.

Her eyes widened. "You think?"

I nodded. "Has to be."

"Wow." She looked at the scarred ground. "So . . . what do we do? Who do we tell?"

"We can't tell anyone without proof. They'd never believe us."

"Yeah, but how do we get proof?"

"He has to be going to wherever he's got the kids hidden away almost every day. Maybe we can follow him."

Since we were thirteen and therefore had neither a car nor driver's licences, and the odds were good he would drive out of town to wherever our classmates were tucked away, it didn't sound like much of a plan, even to me. But it was something.

"Maybe," Meg said doubtfully. "Do you know where he lives?"

"No idea. Let's go find out."

Maybe the ride up here was worth it after all, I thought as we retrieved our bikes and headed back down the hill.

Assuming I survived it. Going uphill, I'd looked forward to going downhill but going downhill, I could only think one thing:

I really need to get my brakes fixed!

CHAPTER 8
I FOLLOW THE VICE-PRINCIPAL

I was just as breathless when we reached the bottom of the mountain as I had been from lack of oxygen during the ascent. (Twelve near-death experiences will do that to you.) We clearly needed sustenance after our gruelling journey, which we found at (where else?) The Dog Pound.

My treat, again. Meg didn't seem to have any money. (I wouldn't have any, either, if this kept up.) Over a pair of Stray Dog Specials (different toppings every day—today it was guacamole, salsa, and crunched-up taco chips, which made me wonder if the owner was just using up leftovers from his weekend TV-streaming binge), we discussed how we could find out where Mr. Reiniger lived.

I'd already checked the town directory on my phone. It listed a number but no address. "We could just call him up and ask him," Meg suggested, but neither of us really liked that idea. For one thing, what possible excuse could *we* have for calling the vice-principal during the summer holidays? Kids just don't *do* that sort of thing. If he *was* Paracelsus, that might tip him off we suspected him, and then who knew what he'd do to Lorenzo and the others?

We could go to the school office and ask where he lived, but that would be even weirder and just as likely to tip him off since Mrs. Petersen, the school secretary, would undoubtedly tell Mr. Reiniger about us asking about him in one of those you'll-never-believe-what-happened-today grown-up small-talk convos. Again, might be bad news for Lorenzo and the others.

We could ask around town, but—same risk. So instead, we settled on a properly Nancy-Drewish plan: hide near the school until Mr. Reiniger left and then follow him home. It was Wednesday, and school was due to start Tuesday. That meant teachers were already there, preparing for the impending influx of bright young minds thirsting for knowledge . . . and the other ninety-five percent of the student body.

Trouble was, it was already three in the afternoon. The teachers would be gone before we could get to the school. Which meant we'd have to wait one more day.

"Maybe that's okay," I said. "We need to talk to Lorenzo again if we can. And Dr. Ballard, too. Want to stay over one more night?"

"Yes," Meg said, real fast.

I blinked. "Don't you have to ask . . .?"

"Mom'll let me," Meg said. "Let's go by my house. I'll leave a note. And pick up some fresh clothes."

So, from The Dog Pound, we cycled . . . slowly, since we were still digesting tubular meat and oil-soaked potatoes . . . to her house. No TV van lurked outside in search of "Eyewitness News," so this time, we headed to the front door.

Meg hesitated on the step. "I . . . guess you can come in?"

I could tell she didn't really want me to. "I'd better wait out here. Keep a look out for roving camera crews."

She gave me a quick, grateful smile, then slipped inside. As the door opened and closed, I glimpsed a living room cluttered with piles of paper, dirty dishes on a coffee table in front of a threadbare couch, pizza boxes on the couch itself, and empty beer bottles on the side tables. I pretended I hadn't seen anything, turning away to sit down on the steps and gaze at the quiet street. Maybe I'd get lucky, and Dr. Reiniger would drive by.

He didn't, but Dr. Ballard did.

I recognized his green thirty-year-old Volvo the minute it turned onto the street. I watched as it rolled past, very slowly. Dr. Ballard had his head turned toward the house. Our eyes met, and for a second, he looked startled. But then he gave me a big smile and a wave and accelerated away.

Weird. I didn't know where Dr. Ballard lived, but I was sure it wasn't in this part of town, and Meg's street didn't go from anywhere to anywhere.

Maybe he was visiting someone else in the neighbourhood, I thought.

Then I frowned. *Or checking up on Meg?*

Well, why not? He might be worried about her, wondering how she was holding up. He might even know what kind of home life she had and figured maybe her mom wasn't exactly providing the kind of emotional support she might need.

The thought made me smile. *Good old Dr. Ballard.* I'd always liked him.

Meg emerged a minute later, carrying a bag. I told her about seeing Dr. Ballard.

"Yeah," she said. "I've seen him on the street a few times. Kind of creepy."

"I think he's being nice," I protested. "Checking up on you."

"Maybe," she said. "But he never talks to me. Just drives by." She picked up her bike from where it leaned against the porch. "Your place?"

"Let's go by the school, just in case," I said. "Maybe we'll get lucky."

We didn't, though. The school—a hundred-year-old three-story brick pile, although the top floor was abandoned and off-limits because the town didn't have enough kids anymore to use all that space—was locked and empty. No cars waited in the parking lot. The only signs of life were two toddlers and their mothers in the playground, shrieking (the toddlers, not the mothers) as they went down the slide.

Meg sighed. "Starting next Tuesday, we're stuck in there again."

"I have a deep, dark secret," I said. Meg raised an eyebrow at me. I shrugged, a little embarrassed. "I kind of *like* school."

She snorted. "I don't. I hate school. *All* schools, not just this one. You would, too, if you'd had to change them every few months."

I thought about how awful that would be: new house, new people, new teachers, new town. I remembered what Meg had said about not even trying to make friends since she knew she'd likely just have to leave them again within a few weeks or months.

Then I thought about how I hadn't made any effort to make friends with her, either, and felt bad. And then I thought about how many of my friends had vanished when the bus crashed and felt worse, although by that point, I wasn't sure if I was feeling sorry for Meg, for myself, for my classmates, or for all of us.

I didn't like feeling sorry for myself. *Feeling sorry for yourself is a waste of time*, Dad told me after Mom died. *Deal with what happened and move on.*

Great advice, although considering how depressed he'd been for months after Mom's funeral, he hadn't been very good at following it.

"We'll come back in the morning," I said. "Let's go to my place. I'll introduce you to *Full Metal Alchemist Brotherhood*. Maybe we'll learn something,"

We didn't—except that you should never try to use alchemy to resurrect your dead mother unless you want your brother to end up as a disembodied soul in a suit of armour and you're not terribly attached to your own legs and arms (honestly, you should *totally* watch it)—but it passed the time until Dad came home. He looked exhausted, so I made spaghetti for all of us, and then we watched an old science fiction movie he liked, and I pretended I liked (Meg was really good about it, too), and then we all went to bed.

Except Meg and I didn't go to bed, of course. This time, we didn't even get undressed. We set up a watch schedule. I'd watch for two hours, then wake up Meg, then she'd watch for two hours, and that way, we could watch all night.

I thought for sure Lorenzo would show up about the time he had the last two nights, around two a.m., which was when I took over from Meg for my second watch . . . but the forest out behind the barn remained dark. I woke Meg at four, sprawled on the bed, and fell instantly asleep . . . and the next time I woke up, it was light. Meg was curled up in her sleeping bag on the floor. I checked the clock. Ten in the morning. Dad must have gone out without waking us. Just as well he hadn't looked in and seen us still in our clothes.

As I swung my feet over the side of the bed, Meg stirred, rolled over, blinked blearily up at the ceiling for a second, and then turned her head toward me. "I stayed up until the sun came up," she said. She yawned and stretched. "He never showed."

I shot the window a worried glance. "I hope nothing bad has happened to him."

"You mean worse than being imprisoned by a centuries-old lunatic and turned into a fire elemental by some process that makes him feel so awful he throws up?" Meg said dryly.

"You know what I mean," I said, turning to her almost angrily. "He could be . . ." I didn't finish that sentence. I couldn't. *He's not*, I told myself fiercely. *He's* not!

I jumped to my feet. "Cereal. And then let's get down to the school and see what we can find out about Reiniger."

"Sounds like a plan."

It did *sound* like a plan, but it wasn't much of one. We rode our bikes down to the school. We sat on a bench in the park across the street. We stared at the school. It stared back in that sort of skull-like way big buildings have, with the arch of the doorway forming a screaming mouth and the windows on either side looking like empty eye-sockets.

"Now we just wait to see Reiniger?" Meg said.

"Guess so."

"Are we even sure he's in there?"

"He has to be," I said. "School starts Tuesday, and he's the vice-principal."

"Even if he is, if he comes out and gets in his car and drives away, we'll never catch up."

"I think he walks to school. Maybe he'll go home for lunch."

It's amazing how boring it is sitting on a park bench staring at a school. Almost as boring as sitting in a school staring at a park bench. We'd got there about eleven, so at least it wasn't long until lunchtime. Fortunately, I had my smartphone. Unfortunately, I'd forgotten to charge it the night before, what with the staying-up-and-watching thing. I turned it on, saw "Low battery warning" for, like, a second, and then it was as dead as . . .

Something. I didn't want to think about dead things.

I was staring at the ground, watching a beetle aimlessly rooting through the leaf litter, when Meg suddenly whispered, "There he is!"

I looked up. Reiniger stood at the top of the high front steps. He pulled a cigarette out of a pack in his pocket, stuck it between his lips, lit it with the flick of a lighter he took from his other pocket, took a deep drag, and then started down the steps.

A smoker! He *had* to be a villain.

Just as we'd hoped, he didn't head to the parking lot. Instead, he strode to the sidewalk and turned right. We jumped up and followed him, hanging back about half a block. I pulled out my dead phone and stared at the blank screen to provide some cover just in case he noticed we were there, but he never turned around.

Three blocks later, he turned right, down a residential street lined with big spruce trees. We hurried so we wouldn't lose him but needn't have bothered. He went inside a two-story apartment building just around the corner.

So, now we knew where he lived.

We stared at the apartment building. Just like the school, it stared back, although its front door gave it more a look of surprise rather than the school's screaming-skull appearance. Unfortunately, there was no handy park bench here. If we stood there long enough, Reiniger would either look out the window and see us or come back outside and see us. "Come on," I said to Meg.

"What?" she asked, confused, but I was already walking up the sidewalk to the apartment building. She caught up with me as I reached the top of the three steps to the porch. "You're not going to buzz him, are you?"

"First, I'm going to find out which apartment he's in." I ran my finger over the annunciator panel until I found his name. "303."

I looked at the apartment door. *It's probably locked*, I thought. But I reached out and tugged at it anyway . . .

. . . and it opened.

It wasn't hard to see why: at some point, someone had forced the lock with a screwdriver or crowbar, leaving bright gouges in the green-painted metal. *Could* have been a burglar, but in our town, it was more likely a tenant who'd forgotten his key but had a toolbox in his pickup.

"Wait," Meg said, but I didn't: I hurried inside.

To our left, a brown couch squatted against the dark wood panelling of the cramped lobby. In front of the window next to the door behind us, two matching brown chairs crouched on either side of a low, scuffed, and water-ring-marked round coffee table. A yellowing potted plant sat on a lace doily in the middle of the table.

Curtains only a few shades of orange away from Cheeto hung in front of the window, and a matching shag rug covered the floor. To our right, a very creepy print of a giant-eyed child stared down at us from above a row of mailboxes.

Directly across from us, behind a wooden railing, an elevated platform ran left and right into the first-floor hallway. Two carpeted steps led up the platform and to an elevator. Two more prints of giant-eyed children decorated the wall to either side of that. They were even creepier than the one above the mailboxes.

I went up to the elevator, reached for the button, and then stopped my finger an inch shy of pressing it: it would be awful if Reiniger happened to be coming back down again, and when the door opened, we found him staring at us with his cold blue Nazi-eyes.

Instead, something even worse happened.

"What are you girls doing here?" said a voice behind us. I emitted a short, perfectly appropriate exclamation of surprise (which it would be *totally* unfair to describe as a squeak) and spun.

Dr. Ballard stood in the doorway, scowling.

CHAPTER 9
I CHAT WITH MY SCIENCE TEACHER

"Noth . . . nothing," I said, the all-purpose denial of a child caught doing something she shouldn't be doing, complete with a stereotypical stutter.

It worked as well as it ever does, which is to say, not at all. Dr. Ballard's scowl deepened. "Really." He looked at Meg. "You, too? Nothing?"

Meg had her head down so that her hair hung over her face. "A friend of mine lives here," she said, sounding sullen.

Good one, I thought, but Dr. Ballard shook his head. "Try again. This is an adults-only building. No children, no pets." He looked from her to me. "I saw you two outside the school. You followed Mr. Reiniger home." He folded his arms. "Care to explain?"

"It was just a . . . a whatchamacallit . . . a whim," I said. "We saw him leaving, and we wondered where he lived. It's always weird to see teachers outside of school. We were just curious, that's all."

"Why were you hanging around the school at all? Don't tell me you're that anxious to get back!"

I glanced at Meg. She kept her eyes down, not looking at Dr. Ballard.

Weird.

I turned back to the teacher. "Actually, we wanted to talk to you," I said, which was *kind* of true. "But we didn't see your car in the parking lot, so we didn't think you were there."

"I wasn't," Dr. Ballard said. "I drove up as you started off after Mr. Reiniger. That was so strange. I thought maybe *I* should follow *you*. And here I am." He gave me a stern look and wasted another one on the top of Meg's head. "You two should leave the poor man alone."

Huh? Poor man?' "Why poor man?"

"His wife is very ill," Dr. Ballard said soberly. "Dying, in fact. She's at home for now, but they're just waiting for the end. I'm rather surprised he's intending to start the school year, and I doubt he'll finish it, but either way, he doesn't need any strife from you two." He unfolded his arms and pointed to the door. "So, out. If you really need to talk to me, we can do that back at the school."

I tried to catch Meg's eye, but she still wasn't looking. I glanced at the elevator doors again. It seemed unlikely that Reiniger could both be centuries-old Paracelsus and caring for a dying wife. Unless . . .

"Have you ever met Mrs. Reiniger?" I asked Dr. Ballard, as casually as I could, as I accepted his not-quite-a-command-but-more-than-an-invitation to leave the premises. Meg trailed behind, still keeping a close watch on the ground as if daring it to make any sudden moves.

"Yes," he said. "Before her diagnosis. She was at the teacher potluck party last March at Jim Sullivan's place."

My mind boggled on several levels. Teachers partying? At

the principal's house? Laughing and drinking and . . . and dancing . . . and . . . and . . .

I ran out of possibilities and didn't really want the images my mind had conjured up lingering in my brain anyway. I couldn't think of anything more horrifying, and considering I'd seen my best friend turned into a walking bonfire, that was saying something.

I was struck dumb for the time it took us to walk to Dr. Ballard's car, the old green Volvo I had seen him drive past Meg's house earlier that day.

Meg climbed into the back seat, her penetrating regard now focused on the carpeted floor mats, while I joined Dr. Ballard on the cracked black leather up front. We drove back to the school in silence, got out in silence, went into the school in silence, and finally entered Dr. Ballard's silence lab . . . I mean, *science* lab, with its rows of two-person work benches, each centred with a little gas spigot to fuel a Bunsen burner. Racks of test tubes stretched out to the right of the sink in the long counter underneath the tall windows, while ten wooden boxes I knew contained microscopes lined up on the left. Behind Dr. Ballard's desk, at the end of the lab closest to the door, hung the big smart board on which equations and science videos and other such educational staples were projected—at least when it wasn't experiencing technical difficulties, which it seemed to every other day. The two ends of the ordinary blackboard it hung in front of flanked it on either side. At the far end of the classroom rose locked, glass-fronted cabinets containing chemicals, rather gross formalde-hyde-preserved dissection specimens that rumour had it had been in the school since before the Second World War (the milky white eyes of a calf's head stared blankly at me), and a few cloudy, unlabeled containers whose contents were a mystery to everyone, but no one had ever dared open.

Dr. Ballard had taken off his suit coat as we came in and tossed it onto the wooden coat rack by the door. Now, he parked his rear on his desk, folded his arms, and raised an eyebrow in my direction. "All right, then. Here we are. What did you want to ask me?"

I glanced at Meg again. She'd hung back as we entered the school and hadn't really come into the lab at all. Instead she was leaning against the doorsill, eyes still locked on the floor.

During the short drive to the school, I'd decided my best tactic would be "distraught youngster."I hadn't used it for a while, but it had never failed.

So I blinked and swallowed hard, as though what I was about to say was very, very difficult for me, and finally blurted out, "I just don't know how I can be in your class after what happened in the spring!"

Dr. Ballard fell for it. He unfolded his arms and leaned back on the desk while giving me the warm smile I knew so well, the smile that had helped make him one of my favourite teachers. "It's not easy for me, either, Sam," he said softly. His smile faded. "Just being in this room . . . remembering all those faces . . ." He shook his head sadly. "It's very difficult. Very, very difficult."

I'd never have a better opening than that. "I just . . . I can't believe they're gone." I gave him my best puppy-dog eyes. "Maybe if I knew more about what happened . . . what do you remember?"

"Surely you've talked to Meg about it." Dr. Ballard's eyes flicked toward the slouching, gaze-down Meg, the last traces of his smile fading as he did so. In fact, the cliché about "looking daggers" at someone came to mind. "What has *she* told you?"

"She doesn't remember much," I said, which was true. I just didn't mention the part she *did* remember.

"Well, neither do I." Dr. Ballard turned his gaze back to me. "One minute, I was driving. The next thing I knew, the paramedics were bending over me. I realized there'd been an accident, but I couldn't understand what they meant when they told me all the kids had vanished . . . well, all except Meg." Again, there was a strange note in his voice when he mentioned her name. *Distaste* came to mind. He shook his head. "Such a terrible tragedy. I know the police have done all they can, but not a trace of them has turned up . . . it's like a nightmare. A horrible, horrible nightmare I haven't woken up from yet. Maybe I never will."

He certainly sounded sincere. But why did he keep giving Meg dirty looks?

I glanced at her, but she still didn't look up. Instead, she suddenly straightened, turned, and went out into the hall as though she couldn't stand to be in the lab anymore.

Too many memories? Didn't sound like Meg. *What's she up to?*

Dr. Ballard followed my gaze and frowned when he saw Meg had gone. "Is that all you wanted to ask me?" he said, still looking out the door after her.

It's like she's the only one he's really interested in, even though I'm the one who's talking to him.

"No," I said, and he looked back at me, this time with a slightly annoyed look. "This may sound like a strange question, but I was wondering . . . have you ever watched *Full Metal Alchemist Brotherhood?*"

He blinked. "Full metal *what?*"

"It's an anime."

Still blank.

"A Japanese animated TV show?"

He made a disapproving *tsk*. "A cartoon?"

No, I thought, irritated, but "Kind of," I said out loud.

"I'm afraid not. Why do you ask?"

"Well," I said, "there's this character called Hohenheim—"

He blinked, and his eyebrows lifted. "Hohenheim? But he was a *real* alchemist."

"I know," I said. "And in the show, he's my favourite character." (A lie: my favourite character was Alphonse, the younger brother, whose soul is trapped in a massive suit of armour while his body wastes away on the other side of the . . . oh, never mind.) "I started reading up on him—the real one, I mean—but it was very confusing. Like, why did the real guy call himself Paracelsus? And then there was all this stuff about alchemy and the Philosopher's Stone—which I thought was just something from *Harry Potter*—and, well . . . I just wondered if you'd ever heard of him or if you know anything about him."

"Actually, I do," Dr. Ballard said. "I've always had an interest in the history of science."

"But he wasn't a scientist, was he?"

"Only because that term didn't exist yet," Dr. Ballard said. "But, like a scientist, he was dedicated to understanding how the world works. Some people think he understood more than anyone else before him and even understood some things that modern people don't."

His face lit up as he talked. Hohenheim was clearly some sort of hero to him.

Or . . .

I felt a chill.

Could Dr. Ballard be . . .?

I didn't want to believe it. I didn't want to *think* it.

But I was.

"You know, there's a section on the history of science in the curriculum for the coming year," Dr. Ballard said. "Everyone has to do a project on a particular scientist. If you're really interested, you could do your project on Paracelsus. I have some books I'd be happy to loan you."

Okay, that kind of undercut the idea that *he* could be Paracelsus. What kind of centuries-old sorcerer would collect books other people had written about him?

An egotistical one, I thought. *And who would be more egotistical than someone who had outlived everyone else and kept his secret for centuries?*

I mentally gave my head a shake. No, the whole idea was nuts! Dr. Ballard had been the science teacher at our school since I was in kindergarten. If he made a habit out of kidnapping students and turning them into elementals, wouldn't he have done it before now?

I still thought Dr. Reiniger was the most likely suspect. I wondered if his wife was really dying. After all, she could be an accomplice. In fact, the more I thought about it, the more likely it seemed. She'd been fine at the party at the principal's house (I shuddered again), but then she'd mysteriously become ill and disappeared? Seemed awfully convenient.

My eyes widened as I suddenly realized just *why* his wife needed to disappear. *The nurse Lorenzo mentioned! That's his "sick" wife! She's looking after the kids he's got locked up! Meanwhile, he shows his face all over town, so everyone knows he hasn't gone anywhere!*

I desperately wanted to tell Meg. And this conversation wasn't going anywhere anyway.

"That sounds great," I said, as brightly and air-headedly as possible. "I'd better catch up with Meg. Sorry we bothered you! And sorry we followed Mr. Reiniger. We were just bored."

Dr. Ballard smiled. "Not to worry. Once school starts, I promise you won't be bored—you won't have time."

That sounded almost like a threat. A *homework* threat, which is the worst kind.

"Okay!" I said, still full of fake cheer. "Great! Bye!"

I beat it.

I found Meg sitting on the front steps of the school, staring at something in her hand. I caught a glint of gold. I plopped down beside her. "Meg," I said. "I'm sure of it now. Paracelsus is . . ."

"Dr. Ballard." "Mr. Reiniger."

We'd spoken at the same instant. We stared at each other.

"What?" "What?"

"You go first," I said, really fast, so she couldn't say *that* at the same time, too.

She held up her hand and opened her fingers. A tiny golden heart-shaped locket dropped from her palm and hung, twisting and twinkling, from a fine gold chain. "This belonged to Melanie Fillion," Meg said flatly. "She was wearing it the day of the accident."

A clue! I thought, back in Nancy Drew mode. "Where'd you find it?"

She scowled at me. "Dr. Ballard's coat pocket."

So *that's* what she'd been doing over there by the door—going through his pockets. "You're sure it belonged to Melanie?"

"Of course, I'm sure," Meg snapped. "I was at the back. She sat a couple of seats in front of me. She came down the aisle, and I saw this locket dangling around her neck, and I thought . . . how pretty it was, and how I wished . . ." She paused for a second, and I saw the muscles in her jaw clench. "How I wished *I* had something that nice. *Anything* that nice."

Her hand closed on the locket. "She was wearing this when we crashed. And Dr. Ballard *had it in his pocket.* That means he knows where she went. That means he's been close enough to her to take it away from her . . . or take it off her body."

I didn't like to think about that second possibility. "You're *sure?*" I said again.

Her closed fist tightened. "Yes, I'm *sure.*"

"In that case . . ." I glanced at the school door. "We should get away from here."

"Not yet." Meg shoved the locket into her pocket. "We need proof he's up to something. Something more than the locket. If we can prove he lied about what happened when the bus crashed, the police will start investigating. They'll find the kids."

I stared at her. "What kind of proof?"

"I don't know. But I know where to look next." She reached into her pocket again, but this time, she pulled out a set of keys: a dozen of them on a ring, from which also hung a car-lock fob.

"You stole his car keys?" I didn't know whether to be impressed or scared. "When he finds out . . ."

"He won't find out. I'll toss them on the ground by his car. He'll think he dropped them there somehow."

"Come on, then!" I jumped up and held out a hand, but she ignored it, getting up on her own. Feeling awkward, I let my hand drop. "If we're going to do this, we have to hurry.

He can't see the parking lot from the lab windows, but he could go into another room if he's suspicious and wants to keep an eye on us."

"He's already been keeping an eye on *me*," Meg said. "I'm probably lucky I haven't disappeared like the rest of them."

We hurried to the parking lot. Dr. Ballard had parked the Volvo with its nose tight to the wall of the school. I looked up. Half a dozen classrooms had a clear view, although it might be hard to look almost straight down and see us. Still, if someone did . . . it wouldn't have to be Dr. Ballard; any teacher in the school would run to get him if they saw kids rifling through his car.

Meg held out the lock fob and pressed a button. With a *clunk,* the car unlocked. *At least it didn't beep.* "We were just inside it," I said. "There's nothing there."

"We haven't seen inside the trunk." Meg moved to the back of the car, reached down, found the latch, and lifted the trunk lid. I ran around to join her.

The trunk contained a small red first-aid kit, some rubber floormats Dr. Ballard probably used in the winter to replace the carpeted ones, two plastic jugs (one of antifreeze, one of windshield-wiper fluid), an empty cardboard box with the words Sumac Ridge Estate Winery printed on it and the very weird word "Gewürztraminer" scrawled across it in felt pen . . . and a paper shopping bag.

"There's nothing strange in here," I started to say—but Meg reached into the bag and pulled out a coat, and the words died in my throat.

I'd seen that jacket every day last spring before the ill-fated class trip. Dark purple, it had "Mountainside Dance Studio" embroidered in gold script on the back.

It had belonged to Melanie . . . just like the locket.

"Hey!"

The shout came from the direction of the school. My heart jumped into my throat and started pounding as though trying to get out of my neck. Meg swore, grabbed the bag, slammed the trunk shut, threw the keys toward the school, and ran.

I dashed after her, sure Dr. Ballard must be hot on our heels . . . but when we reached the other side of the street, and I hadn't heard anything, I glanced back and saw him just standing by his car, recovered car keys in hand, staring after us. I couldn't read his expression from that distance, but I had a hard time imagining it was a happy one.

We grabbed our bikes and pedalled away as fast as we could. I kept looking over my shoulder, expecting to see that green Volvo close behind, but there was no sign of it, and after we'd zigged and zagged and bounced over shortcuts through ravines and parks for twenty minutes, there was no way he could have followed us even if he'd wanted to.

The strange thing was, I didn't get the feeling he'd wanted to.

CHAPTER 10
I EAT A CHILI CHEESE DOG AND VISIT THE POLICE

Somehow, we ended up at the Dog Pound. (Well, it *was* lunchtime, and there's nothing like running for your life —or even just *imagining* you're running for your life—to help you work up an appetite.) We ordered fries to share and a drink and dog apiece (I went with the Coney Island Chili Dog today: sometimes, all you want is a classic), then adjourned to one of the picnic tables.

After a couple of bites took the edge off my famishment, I wiped my fingers on my napkin and asked Meg if I could see the locket. She dug it out of her pocket and held it out. I took it, then used my thumbnail to flick it open.

I found myself looking at a much younger Melanie, the way I remembered her from about Grade 3. We'd been good friends back then but had hardly talked for the last year or two . . . funny how things change.

For some reason, I had to blink hard as I handed the locket back to Meg. She put it on the table next to her half-eaten Chipotle Bacon Cheese Dog.

"Why'd you go through Dr. Ballard's pockets?" I asked her.

"Because I've been suspicious about him ever since it happened,' she said. "It seemed weird, him being left in the bus after all the kids were gone. And then, there's all that creepy driving past my house. I just didn't have a clue what he could be up to. Now I do."

"You think he's Paracelsus."

"Don't you?"

"No," I said. "I think it's Dr. Reiniger."

"What about his sick wife?"

"That's *why* I think it's him," I said. "Lorenzo mentioned a nurse, right? Reiniger . . . Paracelsus . . . needs someone to look after the kids while he stays in town and lets people see him. That way, nobody suspects anything." I pointed a French fry at her. "She's not really sick. That's just an excuse so she could disappear, and people would leave him alone. She's wherever Lorenzo and the others are."

"But what about the locket?" Meg said, almost angrily. "What about the jacket?"

"Maybe the locket came off in the crash, and Dr. Ballard just picked it up. Maybe he found the jacket . . . or maybe it got left behind. Maybe he means to give them to her parents."

"Then why hasn't he?"

"They're away," I said. "They've been away all summer. I'm not even sure . . . they're coming back." I had to swallow a lump in my throat: I'd had a sudden flashback to sitting at the Fillions' kitchen table having hot cocoa and cookies with Melanie when we were about eight after we'd gone sledding on a snowy winter day.

"Maybe that's true," Melanie said scornfully. "And maybe when I wake up in the morning, my room will be full of unicorns." Her eyes narrowed. "What did you talk to him about after I left the lab? Me?"

"No!" *Paranoid much?* "Paracelsus."

"And?"

"Well . . ." I was still trying really, really hard to hold on to my Reiniger Hypothesis, but thinking back to that strange conversation, it suddenly started to sound pretty flimsy, even to me. "Um . . . Dr. Ballard is kind of a . . . a fan. Knows all about him. Has books and everything . . ."

My voice trailed off in the cold light of Meg's narrow-eyed stare. I sighed. "Okay, you're right. Dr. Ballard wins the 'Most Likely to Be An Ancient Undead Alchemist' award." I tried to smile. "Wasn't it Dr. Ballard who told us last year that 'many a promising hypothesis has been slain by an inconvenient fact?'"

"Must have been before I got here. Or else I was asleep." Meg shoved the locket back into her pocket and picked up her root beer (I'd ordered iced tea myself). These dogs, drinks, and fries, hard on the heels of my previous feedings of Meg, had exhausted my meagre stash of cash. I'd have to hit Dad up for an advance on next week's allowance if we wanted to keep using the Dog Pound as our mini-Scooby Gang hideout.

(Not that I've ever seen *Scooby Doo*, but I *did* stream all of *Buffy the Vampire Slayer* when I was ten, so I knew the reference. Again, Dad never knew. I only had a couple of nightmares . . . okay, maybe three . . . so it was all good.)

"But it doesn't make any sense," I said, telling Meg what I'd already thought while I was talking to Dr. Ballard. "He's been at the school as long as I have. How could he be Paracelsus? In all those years, no *other* kids have gone missing."

Meg shrugged. "Maybe he only does it every few years. If

he's Paracelsus, he's centuries old. He can afford to be patient."

She was making way too much sense (if suggesting our science teacher was a centuries-old sorcerer could be said to make *any* kind of sense). I wished she wasn't. "I don't want it to be him," I said, and even I could hear the little-kid whininess in my voice. "I *like* Dr. Ballard. He's always been one of my favourite teachers. Even before I had him for science. He's nice to everyone."

"He was nice to me, too, before the accident," Meg said. "But did you see the way he looked at me in the school? Being nice is all an act. And he's had years to practice it, just to set up . . . whatever he's doing now."

I felt a little sick to my stomach. And then I felt the first stirrings of anger. If this were true . . .

"What do we do about it?"

"I told you at the school," Meg said. "We go to the police."

I was chewing my last French fry. It suddenly tasted like sawdust. I tossed the last little piece back into the basket. "They won't believe us."

"We have the coat."

"But we can't prove it was in Dr. Ballard's trunk. They might think we're just trying to get him in trouble because he gives us too much homework." I gestured from me to her. "We're just kids. He's a respected schoolteacher. Why would they believe us?"

Meg looked stubborn. "We have to try."

I wanted to say, *No, we don't*, but I couldn't. She was right.

I sighed and got to my feet. I picked up our dog- and fry-baskets and ketchup-stained paper napkins and my empty iced tea bottle. "Then we'd better do it now—before he reports us for breaking into his car."

"We didn't break in. We had the key."

"Which you stole from Dr. Ballard's coat pocket," I pointed out. "I'm sure *that* will convince them we're on the up-and-up."

"Are we going or not?" Meg said, looking and sounding stubborn.

"We're going." I tossed the plates and bottle into the nearest trash receptacle (the Dog Pound was not the kind of place to bother with a recycling bin). Meg threw her root beer bottle in after them. A half-dozen angry wasps rose up in response. Stirring up a wasps' nest seemed like an awfully bad omen, considering we were about to accuse a respected junior high teacher of . . . something.

Not that I believe in omens.

Much.

Limberpine Police Headquarters occupied a two-storey brick building on Main Street, next to the public library and across from the town hall. Meg and I shoved the front wheels of our bikes into the bike rack in front of the library, then walked up the steps of the police station, Meg carrying the shopping bag containing Melanie's coat. Two huge black wrought iron lamps, each topped by a frosted-glass ball with the word POLICE printed on it, hung on either side of the big glass double doors. Gold letters on the doors spelled out the same ominous word, just in case you hadn't got the message.

I'm not saying we were intimidated, but we stopped dead for a second. Just to get ready. "Are you sure about this?" I said to Meg.

Her lips tightened. "I'm sure." She reached out for the big brass handle on the right-hand door and pulled it open.

We stepped through into a long, marble-floored hallway with an arched ceiling, lit by a series of frosted-glass spherical light fixtures hung on long chains. There were closed doors to our left and right. At the far end, a counter spanned two-thirds of the hallway. It had yet another glass globe lamp with the word POLICE on it, this one set on a post on one corner. Past the counter, through an open door, I could see into a big room, where I glimpsed a couple of uniformed cops, a man and a woman, sitting at desks and talking on phones.

Behind the counter sat Sergeant Smithers, and I suddenly felt better. Sergeant Smithers came to the school every year to talk about bicycle safety. I'd known him for years. Pudgy and bald, he wore round spectacles and smiled a lot. If only he'd had a big white beard, he would have been a dead ringer for Santa Claus—which was why he played Santa in the children's ward of the hospital every Christmas.

"Hi, Sergeant!" I said brightly, giving Meg a significant look that was meant to convey, "Leave this to me."

But Sergeant Smithers did not smile the way he'd always smiled at me before. In fact, he scowled. I'd never seen him do that and it literally stopped me in my tracks, so suddenly that Meg ran into me.

"You two," he said, in the same tone he might have used after stepping on dog poo on the sidewalk.

"Sergeant?" I said warily.

"The chief wants to see you."

I exchanged a glance with Meg. *I knew it*, she mouthed silently. Which put her one up on me. "Um . . . okay?"

Sergeant Smithers lumbered to his feet and came out from behind the counter via a swinging door. "Follow me."

Silently, we followed him. He led us through the big room —the two cops I'd already seen through the door were the only people in it, even though there were eight desks—and to another door at the back, set in a wall of frosted glass. He opened it partway and stuck his head in through the crack. "They're here, Chief."

"Send them in, Sergeant," said a deep voice.

I'd seen Chief Mollard in the distance at parades. He was a big man. That booming voice fit my mental image of him and made me swallow hard.

Sergeant Smithers pushed the door open wide and stepped aside, pointing into the office. I gave Meg a look that might have had just a *touch* of panic in it, and then we entered the lion's den, me in front.

Chief Mollard sat behind an ancient wooden desk that must have been in that office since the building was built. There were two chairs on our side of it. One was empty.

The other held Dr. Ballard.

I stopped so suddenly Meg ran into me again. "Samantha MacReady?" said the chief. He glowered at me. "Margaret LeBlanc?" His eyes, white in his dark-skinned face, switched to Meg. "What's in that bag, Margaret?"

"It's Meg," Meg said. Her eyes flicked to Dr. Ballard. "And *he* knows what's in it. Ask him."

"No need," Dr. Ballard said. "I already told him." He glanced at the chief. "As I should have a long time ago, had I only remembered I had it."

The chief made a dismissive gesture. "Nothing to worry about, Dr. Ballard." His gaze flicked back to us, and his eyes narrowed. "But *you* two have some explaining to do."

I could sense hot anger rising in Meg, as though she, like Lorenzo, were about to burst into flame. I decided I'd better say something first. "You have to admit it looked suspicious," I said. "Dr. Ballard having that locket, I mean. Meg found it lying on the floor under his coat when we went into the school" (I hoped neither my face nor my voice betrayed my lie) "and she took Dr. Ballard's car keys after that because if he really had had something to do with what happened to our friends, well, we couldn't just ask him, could we, because that might be dangerous—what if he made us disappear, too? —and we thought we could get the keys back into his pocket before he noticed, but then when we opened the trunk we found Melanie's coat, and then Dr. Ballard came out and caught us, and . . . " I let my voice trail away. "And here we are," I finished lamely.

Dr. Ballard did the last thing I expected. He laughed. "Oh, Sam," he said, "you read too many kid-detective books."

Actually, aside from my brief *Nancy Drew* phase, I *never* read kid-detective books, but I just nodded and tried to look shamefaced.

Dr. Ballard turned to Meg. "And you," he said. "Honestly, Meg. I knew you were in the back of the bus. If I'd made the others disappear, I wouldn't have left you there."

"*Did* you know I was back there?" she said. "I lay down in the back seat after you started driving. If you'd looked in the rear-view mirror, you never would have seen me."

"I saw you get on the bus, and I knew how many kids were on it," Dr. Ballard said. There was an edge in his voice that belied his jocular tone of a moment before.

Meg said nothing.

"So . . . why *did* you have the locket and coat, Dr. Ballard?" I said.

He sighed. "Nothing nefarious. I took Melanie's coat from the wreck the night of the accident—I was cold, and it was handy. I had it around my shoulders when they took me to the hospital. They shoved it into a bag with some other stuff. I took that bag home when I was released, but between the shock and the media frenzy and the police . . . I forgot I had it. Then, I was gone most of the summer. I came home last week and only found the coat again on Monday. I found the locket in one of the pockets and put it into my own coat pocket to keep it safe. I was going to take both to Meg's parents when I left the school today . . . but apparently, they're not in town."

"Did you check that?" Meg demanded of the chief.

He frowned at her. "Be respectful, young lady," he rumbled. "Yes, I checked it. They went on an extended vacation with their other two children. After everything the family has been through . . . I think they felt they needed to get away."

I felt silly. My earlier conviction Dr. Ballard couldn't possibly be Paracelsus rushed back. I looked sheepishly up at Dr. Ballard. "I'm sorry," I said. "It's just . . . it seemed so odd, and . . ."

He gave me the warm smile I'd always loved. "Not to worry, Sam," he said. "You had the best of intentions. But don't let your imagination get the better of you. You live in the real world, not in some fantastic kids' book."

I'm not so sure about that, I thought, remembering fire-Lorenzo flickering in the forest, but I didn't say anything out loud except, "Yes, sir."

Dr. Ballard glanced at Chief Mollard. "If that's all, Chief, I really need to get back to the school. I've still got some work to do today. Classes start on Tuesday!"

Chief Mollard nodded. "Of course, Dr. Ballard. You're free to go."

Dr. Ballard smiled at me, frowned at Meg, and then went out.

"Can we go, too?" I said in a small voice.

"Yes," Chief Mollard said. "But keep that imagination of

yours in check, young lady. Not everyone would be as understanding as Dr. Ballard."

"I will," I said.

Meg said nothing. If anything, she radiated more fury than before.

We beat it. "You okay?" I said to her once we were outside.

"No," she snapped. "I'm not." She grabbed the handlebars of her bike and jerked it upright. "Dr. Ballard is lying."

I chewed on my lip as I lifted my own bike. Inside, I'd been willing to accept Dr. Ballard's excuses. But Meg was so sure . . .

"Let's say I believe you," I finally said.

Meg, straddling her bike, glared at me. "Are you saying you don't?"

"I'm saying the jury is out. Which means we need more evidence. Which means our plan hasn't changed, except now it's aimed at Dr. Ballard instead of Mr. Reiniger. We have to follow him. If he took our friends, he'll lead us to them."

Meg glowered at me. "*Your* friends. I told you, I barely knew them."

"Fine," I snapped, my own patience wearing thin. "*My* friends." I mounted my own bike. "But the big problem with this 'plan' hasn't changed, either. If he has them, he must have them hidden somewhere outside of town—there's no way they could be anywhere in Limberpine without someone noticing something. That means he drives wherever it is. It could be miles. We're thirteen. We can't drive."

Meg smiled . . . well, she showed her teeth. "We can't drive *legally*."

I blinked. "What?"

That predatory grin widened. It made her look like a wolf. "I know how to drive."

I blinked again. "What?" I repeated.

(Look, I'd love to engage in witty banter all the time—like on *Buffy*—but unlike *that* Scooby Gang, I don't have a scriptwriter.)

"Last town we were in, we lived in an old farmhouse out in the country. There was nobody around, so Mom taught me to drive out there."

"Why?"

She looked down at the ground. "She just did."

"But . . ."

Her face came up. "So I could come get her from the bar when she was drunk!" she snapped. "Happy?"

My face burned. "I'm sorry. I didn't . . ."

"Drop it." She was gripping her bicycle handlebars so tightly that her knuckles had turned white. "How long do the teachers stay at the school on these getting-ready days?"

"I'm not sure," I said, glad to change the subject.

"Then we have to move fast." She put her right foot on the pedal. "Mom walks to work. Our car's on the street in front of the house. And I know where the keys are."

"That's a relief," I said, but actually, I felt pretty much the direct opposite of relieved. I pasted a fake grin onto my face. "I was afraid you were going to tell me we'd have to hotwire it."

"I know how to do that, too," Meg said and pedalled away.

Why am I not surprised? I thought and followed.

I spent most of the ride to her house trying to convince myself this was a good idea. At least Meg was tall, so she'd be able to see over the wheel and reach the pedals. She might even pass for sixteen if the only glimpse people had of her was through the windshield (and it was dirty enough). If she really did know how to drive, and was careful, there was absolutely no reason she should attract the attention of any cops.

Well, unless that cop already knew who she was, and knew she was only thirteen, and happened to see her drive by, and then stopped her and arrested her, and then hauled me in too, and then I had to call Dad . . . he'd ground me until I was eighteen and who would help Lorenzo then . . .?

I took a deep breath. *One thing at a time. First thing, ride our bikes to Meg's house. Second thing . . .*

Second thing, stop at the corner of the block and stare at the TV van, once again parked right across the street.

CHAPTER 11
I CREATE A DIVERSION

Parked on the opposite side of the street from the TV van, and just a little farther down, was a rusty Chevy station wagon at least twice as old as me. "Your Mom's?" I said, pointing at it.

Meg nodded.

I sighed. I had a very low opinion of TV reporters, but it did not seem likely even they could be clueless enough to fail to notice the thirteen-year-old girl they were hoping to interview get into a car and drive away.

We studied the situation. "I can get into the house from the back and get the key," Meg said, "but there's no way I can get in the car without them seeing me."

"What we need," I said, channelling all the adventure movies and TV shows I'd ever watched, "is a diversion."

Meg gave me a skeptical look. "Like what?"

"Leave that to me," I said, with more confidence than I felt. I had an idea, but I also had a more-than-niggling suspicion it wasn't a *great* idea. It was the only one I had, though, and we needed to get back to the school before Dr. Ballard came out, or we'd have to wait at least a day to try it again, and I didn't know if we had a day. Lorenzo hadn't come back the night before. That worried me. It worried me a *lot*.

So what if my "diversion" might break my neck? A small price to pay to save Lorenzo!

"Go get the key," I said. "Turn the front porch light on and off when you're ready."

She gave me another I-hope-you-know-what-you're-doing-but-I-doubt-it narrowed-eyes look, then turned her bike and rode down the cross-street to the alley.

I couldn't see her once she turned in behind the trees in the alley, so I watched the front porch. It seemed to take forever, but eventually, the yellow bulb above the door flicked on and off. I wondered if the TV crew had seen it. It didn't matter. I was about to give them something else to focus on.

I pushed off from the curb, stood up on the pedals, and pumped as hard as I could, driving the bike faster and faster. The TV van swelled in size. I zipped past it, caught a glimpse of a startled white face looking out the right passenger window—and then turned sharply left in front of the van, yanked up on the handlebars to jump the curb, flew across the sidewalk, jerked the handlebars sideways, and jumped.

I figured it would look like I'd crashed. I figured I could roll when I hit the grass and probably not hurt myself too much. Of course, the key words in that "plan" were "probably" and "too much." And "probably" for some definitions of "too much," I didn't really "hurt" myself. But I hit a lot harder than I'd imagined in my head, rolled a lot farther, and banged my back into a sprinkler head I hadn't realized was there, and then lay there gaping like a landed fish because I'd knocked out my breath.

Still, as a diversion, it was first-rate. Both the van's front doors and the sliding door on my side opened, and the entire TV crew—a female anchor person, a big burly guy with a beard who seemed to be the driver, and a young goateed cameraman—jumped out and ran over to me.

"Are you all right, kid?" boomed the bearded driver.

"Are you hurt?" the anchor-woman said breathlessly.

"I wish I'd caught that," said the goateed camera guy. "Bummer."

I managed to draw a tiny, painful breath and waved my hands around, all the answer I could manage.

"Anything broken?" said bearded-driver.

"Are you bleeding?" said anchor-woman.

"Totally awesome," said camera-guy.

Behind them, I saw Meg come out the front door and run to the station wagon. I managed just enough breath to groan loudly as the car started up. None of them turned around.

"Can you talk?" said bearded-driver.

"What's your name?" said anchor-woman.

"Totally rad," said camera-guy. "Can you do it again?"

The Chevy rolled down the street and turned left, vanishing from sight.

My breath was back. More or less. "I'm okay," I half-lied. (Maybe more than half.) "Thanks."

I sat up. I felt a little sore—okay, a *lot* sore where I'd hit the sprinkler head—and a little shaky, but nothing seemed to be broken, and I wasn't bleeding, so win!

"Sorry," I said. "My bad."

"What's your name?" anchor-woman repeated.

"Abbie," I said, pulling a name out of my head randomly and, apparently, alphabetically. "Abbie . . . Winters. I'm okay." I got to my feet. The driver grabbed my arm and helped me up. I let my eyes drift to the van. "You're a TV crew," I said.

"Why are you sitting here?" I looked across at the house. "Who lives there?"

They exchanged glances. "Probably shouldn't say," said the anchor-woman.

I shrugged and used my best teen-smart-aleck voice. "What*ever*." I looked for my bike, found it, and picked it up. It looked undamaged—unlike me. I was going to have a couple of spectacular bruises in places I didn't know anyone else well enough to show. "Thanks again."

"Are you *sure* you're all right?" said the driver. "Did you hit your head? Maybe we should take you to the hospital, get you checked out . . ."

"I didn't hit my head," I said hastily. Meg must be almost at the school by now. Assuming she really could drive and hadn't run into a tree. "Got to go. Thanks!" I mounted the bike and rode away before they could decide to stop me.

At the corner, I stopped and looked back. They had piled back into their van and resumed their watch on Meg's house. Since nothing was going to happen there, in a way, I'd done them a favour by livening up an otherwise really boring afternoon.

Grinning—and wincing once in a while—I pedalled back to school.

CHAPTER 12
I WEAR UGLY SUNGLASSES DURING A CAR CHASE

Meg had parked her mom's car half a block from the school, close enough to keep an eye on Dr. Ballard's Volvo in the parking lot but not so close it would look like we were conducting a stakeout, even though that was totally what we were doing.

At least, it wouldn't look like that if he didn't see us sitting there. Which is why, once I'd shoved my bicycle into the back of the station wagon and climbed into the passenger seat beside Meg, I scrunched down as far as I could. "What if he recognizes the car?" I said to Meg, who was scrunched down already. Then I blinked. "Where'd you get the sunglasses?"

"Glove compartment. And to answer your first question, if he recognizes the car, we're screwed."

"And you can really drive?"

"I got it here, didn't I?" she said. "Lots of farm kids learn to drive pickups when they're, like, ten or eleven. There's nothing special about being sixteen."

Well, except for the not-getting-arrested part, I thought.

We sat there, waiting. Nothing happened. For a long time. A *very* long time.

In my defence, I'd been up late every night recently, thanks to Lorenzo. So, it was totally not my fault I fell asleep.

I woke to the sound of Meg starting the engine. For a second, I didn't know where I was. Then I remembered and jerked upright.

"Down!" Meg said. At some point, she'd put on a ludicrous straw gardening hat—it must have been in the back seat and presumably belonged to her mom. "He's just getting into his car. He won't recognize me, but he'll spot you right away."

I barely recognized her, and I was sitting right next to her, so I couldn't argue with that. I crouched down on the floorboards. Not putting on my seatbelt went against years of parental indoctrination, but I figured I had a good excuse this time. As long as Meg didn't run into anything . . .

Although, since Meg was as illegal a driver as she could possibly have been without also being drunk, that might not be a safe bet.

All the same, I stayed there, looking up at Meg. I heard a car drive past. "He's at the corner, turning right," she said. We started to move. "You can come up now."

I scrambled up into the passenger seat and buckled my seatbelt with a huge sense of relief. "There's a spare pair of sunglasses in the glove compartment," Meg said. "Put them on."

I opened the glove compartment and pulled out one of those clunky wrap-around pairs of sunglasses old people wear to protect their eyes from UV radiation. "Really?"

"They belonged to my grandma," Meg said. "Can you

think of a better disguise? No kid would be caught dead wearing them."

If you crash, I'll be caught dead wearing them, I thought, but I put them on. The world took on a deep blue-green tint as though we were underwater. I saw Dr. Ballard's car about two blocks ahead of us, heading away from downtown. In fact, the road he was on would take him—and us— completely out of the town in about a mile and a half.

I glanced at Meg. She stared straight ahead, both hands on the wheel, the tip of her tongue protruding between her teeth. She looked totally focused and totally in control, both of which seemed like good things in a driver.

I kept looking left and right and then twisting around to look behind us, keeping an eye out for a) people who might recognize us and call the cops or b) the cops. But I didn't see anyone except a little blonde-haired girl I didn't recognize, walking along the curb with one foot on the street and one in the grass, lost in her own world. She didn't even look up as we passed.

As we approached the edge of town, Meg suddenly pulled over. I glanced at her. "He's still going."

"Yeah," she said. "And if we follow him too closely, he'll know we're following him."

"But we'll lose him."

"We'll wait until he's almost out of sight and then keep going," Meg said.

I looked at her. "You act like you've done this before."

"No," she said. "But I watch a lot of TV."

"On TV, they practically tailgate people, and they only get noticed if the plot requires it."

"Exactly," she said. "I learned how to do it *wrong* from TV. I'm going to do it right."

"If you say so." I took off the awful sunglasses and blinked in the brightness. Dr. Ballard's car was dwindling up the road, which ran east, straight as an arrow. The late afternoon sun made his rear window sparkle like a diamond.

Very late afternoon sun. "What time is it?" I said, suddenly uneasy.

"I don't know. Late. He stayed in the school forever."

I groaned. Dad must be home and wondering where I was . . . and my phone was still dead, having not magically recharged itself since that morning. There was no way I could make any excuses for being late.

There was no way I could call for help if we needed it, either. Which made me more than a little uneasy.

The sparkle on Dr. Ballard's back window suddenly vanished as the road bent left into the forest. "Now," Meg said, put the car into drive, and accelerated—quite a bit more, and faster, than she had in town.

I gulped and gripped the edge of the seat. "Are you sure this is safe?" I said.

"I'm a good driver," Meg said. "Don't worry . . ."

Even as she said it, we ran over the white line onto the shoulder. She swerved back.

"Hey!" I said. (Okay. *Squeaked.* Satisfied?)

She shot me a wicked grin, and I realized I'd been had. I stuck out my tongue.

I had ridden my bike out here a couple of times. I knew that the road curved around the shoulder of a mountain, turned north, and eventually joined a main highway, although that was thirty miles away. What I couldn't remember was how many side roads there were along the way. If he turned down one of those—and he almost certainly would if he was heading to some sort of secret hideout—then we could easily lose him, trailing this far back.

Of course, he might also just be heading out to go fishing in Brindleback Brook. Or even heading to the highway, starting a longer trip. Truth is, the whole "let's follow him and see where he goes" was beginning to seem even more like a half-baked idea than it had at first (and it had *never* seemed very well-baked), especially with an underage driver at the controls. But we were committed now.

After her ha-ha-look-I'm-losing-control "joke" Meg settled down and drove properly, carefully staying at the speed limit. The road turned into the trees and began to wind, never revealing a straight stretch long enough for us to catch sight of Dr. Ballard's car if it was even still in front of us. We travelled five miles, then ten. Twice, we passed cars going the other way, and both times, I hunkered down while Meg sat up straighter, trying to look as old and tall as possible.

We passed half a dozen side roads, and each time, I wondered if Dr. Ballard had gone down them, but three were blocked by padlocked gates, one just ran a couple of hundred yards to a pond in a meadow, one had been washed out, so that a gaping ravine slashed across it, and one was marked, "Clearwater Bible Camp," a place where I had spent an interminable week once and knew was highly unlikely to be home to a dozen children undergoing alchemical transformations.

And then, completely without warning, Meg braked so suddenly that if I hadn't been wearing my seatbelt (thanks, Dad!) I would have banged my head on the dashboard.

I glared at her. "What was that for?"

"Dust."

"What?"

She pointed left. I looked down yet another side road and

saw what she had seen: dust hanging in the air, catching the last rays of the sun, about to slip behind the mountains. Someone had driven down that road just minutes before.

"It could have been someone else," I pointed out.

"Maybe," Meg said. "But if it wasn't him, he's way ahead of us and heading to the highway, and we'll never catch him anyway. I'm not going to drive on the highway even if we could figure out which way he went."

I heartily approved of *that*. "All right. Let's check it out."

Meg shoulder-checked, then backed up, swinging the rear of the car to the right so the nose pointed left. Then she drove down onto the rutted dirt road and we trundled through the slowly settling cloud of dust into the gathering shadows beneath the trees.

The road was . . . odd. Though it wasn't paved now, it looked as if it might have been at one point but had been dug up. Chunks of asphalt stuck up among the weeds to either side.

That was weird enough. What was weirder was that the road took us through an open gate in a sagging fence—not an ordinary barbed-wire fence, but a tall chain-link fence topped with curly barbed wire—and past what had obviously been a guard house, though plywood covered the windows.

Beyond the guard house, the road ran on through the trees a few more yards, then dipped out of sight.

Meg stopped just inside the gate. "Now what?" I said to her.

"It's a compound of some sort," Meg said. "That means there's something in the middle of it, which is probably down in that hollow in front of us. Which means if Dr. Ballard really did come this way, he's probably parked down there right now. And he could see us the minute we reach the top of the dip."

"Good thinking," I said, impressed again. "We'd better . . ." (more dialogue from movies supplied itself) " . . . reconnoitre on foot."

We got out, leaving the doors ajar because you can't close a car door quietly. We slipped into the woods to maximize the cover for our approach (listen to me, sounding all commando-like). We crept forward to conduct our reconnaissance. (I could get into this.)

But when we got to where the ground sloped, we didn't see what we expected to see. There was no building down there: just an overhanging slab of concrete sticking out of the cliff face on the far side of the little ravine into which the road had plunged. There was no sign of Dr. Ballard, of his car, or of anyone else's car. The place looked deserted.

Except . . . dust hung in the air.

"Somebody drove down there," Meg said.

"There must be a way in under that concrete porch-roof thingy," I said.

"Which means there's a whole . . . something . . . underground?" Meg said. "Weird."

I stared at the concrete porch-roof thingy (well, what would *you* call it?) . . . and suddenly, I knew what it was. "It's a bunker—a bomb shelter!"

"A bomb shelter?" Meg gave me a skeptical look. "Out here? It wouldn't do anyone in town any good way out here."

"It wasn't for anyone in town," I said excitedly. "Dad told me there used to be a, a, a whaddyacallit, a survivalist cult that lived in the woods somewhere outside of town, back in the 1960s. They were very secretive, grew their own food, only came into town if there was something they really, really needed. They thought there was going to be a nuclear war with the Russians, and they were going to stay safe in their shelter and then come out when it was all over, and the fallout had . . . fallen out, I guess."

"But there wasn't a war."

"Obviously," I said. "Or we wouldn't be here. And nobody knows what happened to the cult. Everybody just vanished. The police came out and sealed off the entrance to their shelter, and that was that."

"Looks like someone unsealed it," Meg said.

"Yeah." I felt a shiver. Despite everything, I'd still kind of been hoping that Dr. Ballard wouldn't be our man. But things weren't looking good for that hypothesis.

New hypothesis: Dr. Ballard was Paracelsus and had imprisoned his entire Grade 7 science class from the previous year in an old bomb shelter.

Dr. Ballard himself had taught me that once you had a hypothesis, you needed to design an experiment to test it. Unfortunately, the only way to test this hypothesis that I could think of was to find a way into the bunker.

Which meant abandoning our nice, safe hiding place.

"We have to go down there," Meg said, her thoughts having obviously formed the same uncomfortable train as mine.

However, an even more uncomfortable caboose had just attached itself to mine. "No," I said. "*One* of us should go down there."

"Why . . ." Meg started, then stopped. "Oh. So there's someone to go for help if something . . . goes wrong."

I nodded. "And that means it has to be me."

Believe me, I really didn't want to say that, but it was the only thing that made sense.

"Why . . ." Meg began and again stopped. "Oh. Because I can drive, and you can't."

"Yeah."

Meg looked back at the car, then at me. "You're sure?"

I thought of Lorenzo, locked up and experimented on, and suddenly felt ashamed of my own fear. "Yeah. I'm sure."

There was no point in delaying. I scrambled to my feet, brushed pine needles off my knees, and started down the twilit slope.

Moment by moment, the darkness deepened, good from a making-me-harder-to-see point of view, not so good from an is-there-anyone-or-anything-else-down-here point of view: nymphs, sylphs, salamanders, or mud-men "gnomes," to pick four terrifying possibilities.

But I got down to the level of the bunker without incident. Underneath the concrete porch-roof thingy, I discovered a single garage door set in the middle of a wall of concrete blocks. On either side of the garage door were slotted vents, presumably to ventilate the space beyond.

I stared at the door. I glanced back up the slope and waved in the general direction of Meg, just to show I was all right—although that was subject to change without notice, and I wasn't even sure she could see me in the fading light—then turned back to the garage door.

There was no handle on it, nothing to get hold of. Dr. Ballard probably had a garage-door opener in his car, but there was no way *I* was getting through it short of having Meg ram it with her mother's car, which seemed both drastic and likely futile, not to mention really hard on the car.

I chewed on my lip. I couldn't get inside, and I couldn't see inside. Maybe I could *hear* inside?

I crept—I don't know why I crept; it didn't seem likely

anyone inside could hear me, but still, I crept—up to the nearest vent, to the left of the door. I put my ear to it. Air blew out of it, cold and dank. All I could hear was the hum of whatever fan was doing the blowing.

I crept over to the other vent. Same thing, except this one seemed to be sucking air *in*. Either way, I could hear nothing.

I had just straightened when, suddenly, I *did* hear something, faint but unmistakable, a sound that raised the hackles on the back of my neck and sent a cold shiver down my spine.

I heard a boy's voice.

Screaming.

CHAPTER 13
I MISPLACE MEG

I pressed my ear harder to the metal slats of the vent, but the screaming had stopped, cut off suddenly by what had sounded like the closing of a door. Had I really heard it at all?

Almost desperately, I explored the concrete wall in both directions, but there was no other entrance. I returned to the vents and listened again. Only fan noise for several minutes—and then, garbled and unintelligible voices, one male, one female, followed by the sound of a car door opening and closing.

I jerked upright and turned to run back up the hill to Meg, but it was too late. With a whirring, grinding noise, the garage door began to rise.

There was nowhere to hide, nowhere—and no time—to run. I did the only thing I could and pressed my back to the cold concrete blocks of the wall, heart pounding. In the darkness, maybe, just maybe, Dr. Ballard—if it really was him—wouldn't notice me, either as he drove out or by looking in his rear-view mirror.

Not that that would save us for very long, not once he got

to the top of the hill and saw Meg's mother's car sitting there. Dr. Ballard might not recognize it, but he'd know someone was around. All he'd have to do then was block the gate with his car and search the compound.

And then maybe *we'd* be screaming down inside this old bunker.

Only a faint red light showed beneath the garage door as it ground its way upward, the kind of light that couldn't be seen from very far away. Whoever was about to come out didn't want anyone looking down from a mountainside to wonder why there was a light down here.

Nor did any headlights come on, no doubt for the same reason, and suddenly, I thought I really *might* have a chance of not being seen.

A car nosed out of the garage. I couldn't see it clearly, but the red light did catch the unmistakable emblem on the grill: a circle with an arrow pointing up the right, a strip of metal running diagonally, and one word: VOLVO.

Dr. Ballard!

I dropped to the ground, rolled up against the wall, and pressed myself against it. The front wheels rolled by me, then the rear wheels. I could see, dimly, inside the garage.

And suddenly, I realized I had a chance I might never get again.

On my hands and knees, I scrambled into the garage and scuttled around to the left, out of sight of the door. Red light as the Volvo braked, and I gulped, waiting for the sound of the car door opening . . . but instead, all I heard was the renewed grinding of the garage-door motor. Sitting on the concrete floor, back against the wall, I watched it roll slowly down and thud against the floor. Muffled by the metal door, I heard the sound of the Volvo driving away.

I wondered what Meg was doing up above.

I wondered what *I* was doing, in here.

I scrambled to my feet and looked around.

I'd never seen an emptier garage. No workbench, no old bicycles tucked into odd corners, no boxes, no nothing. Or rather, a whole lot of nothing. Plus a glistening patch of some liquid on the concrete floor where the car had been parked. It was probably antifreeze—I remembered the jug of the stuff in Dr. Ballard's trunk, which probably meant his car had a leak —but in the red light, it looked a lot like blood. I gave it a wide berth as I walked the length of the garage to the only other thing there was to look at: a door.

It was a metal door. It had an aluminum handle. I put my hand on the handle and pressed down.

It was, of course, locked.

I put my ear to it. I both did and *didn't* want to hear the screaming again.

I didn't.

I straightened. I made my hand into a fist and pulled my arm back, planning to pound on the door—and then thought better of it. I'd heard voices, a man's and a woman's. Dr. Ballard had left, but I didn't know if the woman had left with him. She might still be inside the bunker. If she caught me in the garage, with nowhere to run . . .

I let my hand fall. I put my ear against the cold metal again. Just for a moment I thought I heard something . . . not a scream, this time, but a distant shout . . . but I couldn't be sure.

I felt sick. Lorenzo was in there. I was sure of it. And all the other missing kids. I had to help them. But how?

I looked around the garage again. Nothing. No tools. No

way to pry the door open. And even if I could, again, what if someone else was in there?

The police, I thought. *We have to go to the police. This time, they'll have to listen to us. They'll have to check this place out even if they don't believe us. It's their job.*

The police!

Full of purpose, I spun around. Now, I just had to find some way to get out of the garage.

The inside of the garage door was as devoid of handles as the outside had been, but there was, on the wall on the opposite side from where I'd hidden, a two-button switch, green on top, red on the bottom. I hurried over, held my breath, and pushed the top button. If it didn't work . . .

It worked. The door ground upward, but I didn't relax my breath. If Dr. Ballard hadn't driven away . . .

But the Volvo was gone. It was full night outside now, and the faint red light from the garage spilled only a short way out into the darkness, but there definitely wasn't a car there.

The question was, what had happened when he got to the top of the hill? Had he seen Meg's car? Caught Meg? Was he about to jump out of the darkness?

I started to run out, then stopped. The door, having reached the top, had stopped wide open. If Dr. Ballard came back, and that door was open, he'd know someone had been inside and maybe that the police were coming. He'd run for it and maybe do something horrible to the kids before he left.

I went back inside and pushed the CLOSE button. Making a godawful racket, the door started down again. I ducked under it, then faced out into the darkness as the red light dwindled behind me, vanishing completely as the door reached the bottom.

Nobody moved. Nobody shouted. Not Dr. Ballard—and not Meg.

I looked up at the sky. Stars pricked it, but there was no moon. I shivered. It had cooled off a lot since the sun went down. I wished I had a jacket.

I thought about shouting for Meg, then thought better of it. I had no idea if Dr. Ballard was lurking somewhere in the woods. Although if he was, he would have heard the garage door, which meant he'd be on his way.

With that thought, I darted away from the bunker like a startled rabbit. Avoiding the road, I scrambled up the slope, which was a lot harder than coming down it had been. For one thing, starlight in a forest is essentially no light at all. I tripped twice, the second time gasping as I got stabbed in the side by a branch or something—not hard enough to break the skin, but hard enough to hurt and no doubt add another bruise to my growing collection—but eventually, panting, I made it to the top.

I stopped there and listened, trying to quiet my breathing but unable to do anything about the pounding of my heart in my ears. The night was quiet, the air so still there wasn't a sound from the trees. I couldn't hear any cars. I couldn't hear anything at all.

I couldn't stand it. "Meg?" I whispered.

Nothing. No sound, no movement.

I took a deep breath. "Meg!" I shouted.

Still nothing.

I hurried toward the gate.

Meg's mom's car was gone.

I ran up the dirt track to the main road. Panting, I stopped and looked both ways.

Nothing. No cars moved.

I was fifteen miles from town. I'd have to walk all night to get there. I was freezing, I was thirsty, I was hungry, and my phone was dead.

There was nothing for it but to turn right and start trudging along the road. Maybe someone would come along, and I could flag them down for a ride.

The thought was a little worrying. I was a thirteen-year-old girl, all alone on a deserted road. Hitch-hiking was definitely . . . what was that word they used in drug ads? . . . oh, yeah: *contraindicated*. But walking all night didn't appeal either. Not when I desperately needed to get to the police, get them out here, get them to search that bunker . . .

And then I saw it. Off to the right, off the shoulder, in among the trees. A dark shape. Starlight glinted off glass and metal. It looked like . . .

I ran, tripped, stumbled, caught myself, kept running.

It *was*.

Meg's mom's car!

It was upside down, broken glass scattered around it, the roof crushed, the door open. I slammed to my knees and stuck my head inside. "Meg!"

She wasn't there.

I jerked my head out, stood up, stared around into the darkness. "Meg! Meg!" I shouted her name a dozen times, stopping to listen after every shout.

Nothing.

Just like the school bus! I remembered what Meg had said, how the ground had risen up and flipped the bus onto its side. *Mud-men. Earth elementals. Paracelsus.*

Dr. Ballard.

Where was Meg?

A sob gripped my throat. I started running again toward

the town, through the woods alongside the road. I had to get help . . .

I tripped in the darkness, fell headlong. My breath whooshed out of me as I slammed to the ground, just like it had when I'd crashed my bike in front of the TV van. Getting my breath knocked out is my least favourite thing ever, and here I'd managed it twice in one day.

For a long moment, I just lay there, gaping like a landed fish. When at last I could stand, I didn't try to run again. If I broke my neck, who would help Meg?

Who would help Lorenzo?

The road. The road was smooth. I could run on the road.

I hurried to it, then started jogging along it, trying to set a pace I could keep up all night if I had to.

But I didn't have to.

I heard them first: sirens echoing off the mountains. Then I saw them rounding a curve, still miles away down the road, but hurrying toward me: the flashing blue-and-red lights of a police car and behind it, the red lights of an ambulance.

Relief flooded me, so sudden and complete that my knees almost buckled. I stopped and waited, waving frantically, standing in the middle of the road. They hurtled toward me. For a minute, I thought they wouldn't see me, thought they'd run me over if I didn't move, and I tensed to fling myself to the side . . .

But they slowed, stopped. Headlights pinned me. I dropped my arm. Doors opened, slammed shut again. Dark shapes, silhouettes against the light, hurried toward me. "Please," I said to the onrushing figures. "Help me . . ."

Then I was surrounded by people. Two policemen, two paramedics. Someone put a blanket over my shoulders. It felt good. "Were you in the car that crashed?" one of them said.

"No," I said. *Well, not when it crashed.* Then I blinked. *Wait, how did they know there'd been a car crash . . .?*

"Was anyone hurt in the crash?" That was a different voice. I couldn't tell who was talking—a cop or a paramedic. Maybe it didn't matter.

"No," I said. "It's empty." *Meg . . .* "But my friend *was* in it. Meg. She's missing . . ."

"Meg Leblanc?" said the first voice.

I blinked. "You know . . .?"

"Her mom called us. Said her thirteen-year-old daughter had taken her car keys and the car and hadn't come back."

"Are *you* hurt?" said the second voice.

"No . . ."

"Come with me," said the first voice.

I was pulled to the cop car, pushed into the back. I sat there, clutching the blanket, as the car accelerated down the road, the ambulance following.

It wasn't far to the wreck. We stopped. The policemen got out. The paramedics joined them. I would have, too, but there weren't any door handles in the back of the cop car. I watched as they all approached the station wagon, bending over to look underneath just like I had. They straightened. I saw them shouting. I knew they wouldn't get an answer.

The cops came back. One of them opened the back door and gestured for me to get out. I did.

"What happened to Meg?" he said.

"I think Dr. Ballard took her," I said.

"Dr. Ballard?" The cops exchanged glances. "The middle-school science teacher?"

"Yes! He kidnapped . . . all those kids that disappeared last year . . . they're close . . . there's a bunker . . ."

"Whoa, slow down," said the second one. "What are you talking about?"

I tried to explain. How we suspected he'd had something to do with the missing kids. How we'd followed him out here . . . "No, Meg doesn't have a licence, but that's not important now" . . . how we'd tracked him to the bunker, how I'd heard a boy screaming . . .

I didn't use the words "Paracelsus" or "alchemist" or "elementals" because I'm not stupid.

The cops exchanged glances again. "She's talking about the National Rebirth compound," the one on my right said to the one on my left as if I wasn't there.

"That place was sealed up," the other one said.

"Dr. Ballard unsealed it," I said. "The missing kids are there. Prisoners. Take me there. You'll see."

They exchanged glances yet again. "We have to check," said the one on the left.

"Yeah," said the one on the right. He looked at the paramedics, who were standing by. "You'd better come, too," he said. "Probably nothing to it, but just in case—"

Probably nothing to it? I felt a surge of anger. "I'm telling the truth!"

"Nobody said you aren't," said the cop on the left. But I could tell from the way he said it that, inside, that was *exactly* what he was saying. "Get back in the car, and we'll go see for ourselves."

I climbed back in. The door closed. The cops got in the front. We drove down the road.

In the car, it took very little time to cover the distance I'd run so frantically along, maybe half an hour before. We turned onto the side road and rolled through the gate past the boarded-up guardhouse, the ambulance following us. I leaned forward as we neared the spot where the road dipped sharply downward to the bunker and the garage, feeling a huge sense of relief. They'd have some way to get inside. We'd find Lorenzo, all the others...

But as the nose of the car dipped downward and the headlights lit up the place where, less than two hours before, I'd stood and heard a boy screaming through an air vent, I gasped.

There was no sign of the concrete porch-roof thingy. No sign of the concrete block wall. No sign of the garage door. No sign of the air vents.

Instead, there was only a huge, tumbled mass of rock and tangled trees.

The entrance to the bunker had been buried in a massive landslide—along with everything inside it.

CHAPTER 14
I RIDE IN A COP CAR

I stared at that impossible sight, my breath catching in my throat in a half-strangled sob. *Lorenzo . . .!*

The cop car stopped. The ambulance pulled up beside it. The cop in the passenger seat got out and opened the back door so I could get out, too, while his partner approached the landslide and shone his flashlight here and there across the mass of stone, lighting up the parts left in shadow by the headlights of the car and ambulance. The paramedics didn't get out.

I ran up beside the cop, heart pounding. *This isn't possible!* The landslide didn't look recent. It looked like it had been there forever.

"Told you," the cop who had let me out of the car said. "The bunker's been sealed for ages."

"But it wasn't," I said. "Just a couple of hours ago, it wasn't like this. It was . . ." I pushed at the rocks. Of course, they didn't budge. "It was . . ." My head spun. I sat down on a fallen boulder. "It wasn't like this," I whispered.

The cop sighed. "Let's go." He pulled me to my feet. I

didn't resist as he led me back to the car. He opened the door to the back seat, but I stopped before I got in and turned to him.

"It wasn't like this," I said again, stronger this time, the shock fading. *Earth elementals. If they could flip over the bus, flip over Meg's car, they could do something like this, couldn't they?*

And that would mean the bunker and the kids I thought were in it were still there, just temporarily buried. Paracelsus —Dr. Ballard—could have the elementals dig out the bunker any time he wanted to.

I still couldn't say anything to the cops about Paracelsus or elementals. But I could say something about Dr. Ballard. "Maybe I didn't see everything I thought I saw. It was dark," I said stubbornly. "But I know for *sure* I saw Dr. Ballard's car down here."

"Nothing illegal about being down here," the cop said. "The property's not posted, and the gate wasn't locked."

"But why would he . . .?"

"Why were *you* down here?" the cop countered.

"We followed him."

"Because you think he had something to do with the missing kids."

"He *does!*"

The other cop came up at that moment. He snorted. "Chief told us you two came in, made wild accusations, and couldn't back them up."

I thought I could. I stared sickly at that impossible land-slide. "Shouldn't you question Dr. Ballard?"

"He *was* questioned," the first cop said. "After the disap-pearance. Several times." He shook his head. "Give it up, kid. Back when I was in school, students tried to get teachers they didn't like in trouble. Never worked. You think this is going to make your class with him better this coming year?"

But he's not *a teacher I didn't like. He was always my favourite.* "Aren't you even going to *ask* him what he was doing out here?"

"No," the cop said. "Because *he already told us.* He's the one who called in the accident, although he didn't know Meg had been in the car."

I blinked. "What?"

"He likes to explore the countryside," the second cop said. "He came out this way, saw the gate to the old compound was open, and drove in out of curiosity. Poked around until it got dark, drove back again. When he saw the wrecked car, he called us right away, then stopped to see if someone was hurt. When he couldn't find anyone, he was worried someone might have hit their head and was wandering confused in the woods. He called again, offered to drive on into town and get the volunteer search and rescue teams going. He's a member, you know."

I didn't know.

The first cop picked up the story. "Chief said yes, of course." He scowled at me. "So, while you're out here making wild accusations, Dr. Ballard is back in town organizing a search. There'll be carloads of people showing up any minute. They're all going to be looking for Meg . . . now we know for sure she was the one driving the car."

"Would have been looking for you, too, if we hadn't radioed in that we'd found you," the second cop said, matching his partner's scowl. "Your dad was getting worried."

My heart sank. "Dad called the *cops?*"

"Yeah," said the cop. "You two have stirred up a hornet's

nest. I just hope that friend of yours is all right." He pointed into the back seat. "Now get in and wait."

I got in. The first cop got into the passenger seat again. I sat glumly and silently in the back. Out the window, I saw the second cop talking to the driver of the ambulance. A minute later, he came back to the cop car, got in, backed up, swung around, and headed back out to the main road, once again trailed by the ambulance.

At the intersection, we turned right toward the town. I twisted around to look out the back window and saw the ambulance following us, but as we passed Meg's overturned car, it slowed and turned off. The driver glanced at me in the rear-view mirror. "First search teams will be out here any minute," he said. "Paramedics will hang around in case they find her. My guess is Dr. Ballard was right: she hit her head and wandered off. Maybe collapsed somewhere. But don't worry—she couldn't have gone far."

Not if she was walking, I thought. *But if she was carried off . . .*

Dr. Ballard had found the car. He'd stopped. What if he'd kidnapped her? He could have driven her into town and locked her up in his basement while the cops were heading out here.

"You should search Dr. Ballard's house," I said out loud. I knew it was stupid, I knew they wouldn't pay any attention, but I had to say it. "I'll bet he took her."

Both cops gave me a look, one in the rear-view mirror, the other twisting around to look at me directly. "Dr. Ballard's already on his way back out here with the search teams," he snapped. "He drove straight to the volunteer fire department to get the message out. He didn't kidnap anyone." He twisted around again. "Let's get her home," he said to his partner.

"Let her father deal with her. Then we can come back out and help with the search."

"Works for me," said the driver-cop. He reached down to a control panel straight out of *Star Trek* and pushed a couple of buttons. The lights and siren came on, and we raced back to town, flashing and wailing.

I'd never been in a cop car with the lights and siren going. It should have been exciting. But all I could think about was Meg and Lorenzo. *Just because Dr. Ballard went straight to the firehall doesn't mean he didn't have Meg with him before he got there,* I thought. He could have dumped her somewhere, locked her up before he started calling the search and rescue teams. It was all just . . . what was the word?. . . misdirection. *"Look at all the effort he's putting into finding that poor lost girl," everyone will say . . . just like these cops.*

I suddenly thought of Meg's mom. "Did somebody tell Meg's mother what happened?" I asked the cops, shouting above the sound of the siren.

"Tried," the cop on the right shouted back. "No answer at her house. Someone's calling around to the bars."

I winced. She'd called in that her underage daughter had apparently taken her car for a joyride, then she'd left her house . . . and the first thing the cops thought was that she might be in a bar somewhere? Apparently, Meg's family was well-known to the police already. *Never a good thing.*

And then I thought, *And now my family will be known to them, too. They're going to think I'm a troublemaker. Maybe even a juvenile delinquent. Dad . . .*

I quailed a little at the thought of what Dad would say, but then I straightened my shoulders and stuck out my chin. *It doesn't matter what he says. It doesn't matter if he doesn't believe me. I'm not making any of this up. Dr. Ballard is Paracelsus, he arranged the disappearance of the class last year, he's turning the kids into elementals . . . and he's got Meg. And if no one will help me I'll save her and Lorenzo myself.*

Somehow.

A few minutes after we left the crash scene, we saw a line of cars speeding toward us, clearly the search teams the saintly Dr. Ballard had organized. In fact . . .

I twisted around in my seat as the cars zipped by. Leading the pack was a green Volvo.

I jerked back around and folded my arms, scowling. The cop at the wheel glanced at me in the rear-view mirror but didn't say anything.

Five minutes later, we were driving into town. Five minutes after that, we were driving up to my house.

My ferocious determination felt less ferocious and considerably less determined as the door opened, and I saw Dad silhouetted against the hall light. I swallowed hard.

The driver turned off the flashing lights and siren. As the wailing dwindled to silence, the cop in the passenger seat got out, waved at my dad—who didn't move from the doorway —and came around to open the back door. I climbed out to face the music.

The policeman escorted me right to the front steps. "Station let you know we'd found her, right?" he said to Dad.

Dad nodded. His face might have been cast in stone. Scowling stone, like a granite mountain with a thunderstorm hanging over top of it. All that was missing was the thunder and lightning . . . and I figured I'd be getting that in a minute.

The cop let go of my arm. "She's not hurt."

"What about Meg?" Dad asked, speaking for the first time, and sure enough, there was something very much like the growl of thunder in his voice. I shoved my hands into the pockets of my shorts and stared down at my sneakered feet.

"We don't know," the cop said. "Search teams are out there now. Hopefully, she turns up soon." He glanced up at the starry sky. "At least it's a clear night. Moon'll be up soon. Bit chilly, though."

"I hope you find her," Dad said.

"Me, too." A moment's silence. I figured they were both looking at me. I kept my eyes on my shoes. "Well, we'd better be getting back," the cop finally said. "I'll leave you two alone."

I heard him turn to go, and I finally looked up. "You will call us, right?" I said. "If you find Meg?"

The cop glanced over his shoulder. "Sure thing, kid. Good night now."

He returned to the car, slamming the door. The lights spun to life, sending blue and red spots chasing each other over the front of the house, the barn behind it, and the trees. The cops pulled away. As they turned the corner that would take them back the way we'd come, the siren blared once more.

"Samantha," Dad said quietly, and again I was reminded of a brewing thunderstorm. "Come inside."

"Yes, Daddy," I said in a small voice. He stepped to one side, and I walked into the hall, where I hesitated.

"Living room," he said.

I went in and sat down on the couch.

Dad sat in the armchair. "All right," he said. "What the *hell* did you think you were doing?"

That single swear word felt like a slap. Dad only swore when he thought I couldn't hear him. And he'd *never* sworn at me before.

I suddenly felt very small, and scared, and sick. Tears filled my eyes. "I'm sorry."

"Never mind sorry," Dad said. He wasn't yelling. The storm still hadn't broken. I was beginning to wonder if it would. I was beginning to wonder if it might be worse if it didn't. "Just tell me what happened."

So, I tried . . . but without saying anything about the elementals or Paracelsus because I knew he wouldn't believe me unless he saw Lorenzo with his own eyes. And even then . . . Lorenzo's face had been in the fire, clear as anything, out at the campground, and Dad had thrown water into it as though he hadn't seen anything at all. Would he believe me even if he saw what I'd seen? Or would he just rationalize it away?

Maybe I wasn't being fair to him. But whether seeing Lorenzo would have convinced him or not, I was sure that *not* seeing Lorenzo, mud-men, nymphs, or sylphs *guaranteed* he wouldn't believe me.

I didn't lie. I just didn't tell him everything.

"We thought . . . Meg thought . . . she was suspicious of Dr. Ballard, and just because I wanted to know what he knew about . . . about the Tragedy, because I hadn't had a chance to talk to him before, when we saw him going into the school we went in, too . . . and because Meg was suspicious, she felt in his pocket, and she found Melanie's locket, and so she got his keys, too, and when we looked in the trunk of his car we saw Melanie's coat, and then we got scared and thought maybe he really *had* had something to do with everyone disappearing, so we went to the police station but he was there and nobody would believe us and then Meg said, 'Well, if he's made them disappear, he knows where they are, and maybe he's going to see them,' and so we decided to follow him, but he had a car, and we didn't, except Meg's mom did, and Meg knows how to drive, and so . . . so we followed him to that old bunker outside of town the survivalists used to use and . . . and . . . sure enough, he went into it, and I got out of the car, but then he came out again and got into his and I hid and Meg drove off so he wouldn't know we were spying on him and then she didn't come back so I started walking and then I saw she'd crashed and the police came and . . . and when we went to look, the bunker had been buried by a land-slide and so the police didn't believe me and . . . and here I am."

I ran out of words and out of breath. I stopped and waited again for the storm to break.

But again, it didn't.

"Sam," Dad said, his voice quiet but somehow . . . intense. "I know how hard it must be for you, having lost so many friends. I understand you want answers. Everyone in town wants answers. So many families have been torn apart by what happened. It must be even harder for Meg since she was actually *on* the bus, and doesn't know anything more about what happened than anyone else does.

"I understand grief comes out in different ways. When your mother died, I . . ." He swallowed. "Grief made me do things I wouldn't normally do, either."

I remembered some of those things. Getting drunk. Smashing things. Sobbing. Lying in bed all day. It hadn't been a good time for either of us, but I think it was worse for Dad. I was small. I'd missed Mommy, but I'd still had my daddy. Now . . . I could still remember her, but not as well as I would have liked. In my mind, she was like an . . . an out-of-focus photograph. But for Dad, she must always be there, in the corner of his eye, in his mind and heart.

Except, of course, she wasn't there at all, and she would never be there again.

I'd thought Lorenzo was gone forever, too. But he wasn't, not yet. Although he might be soon.

Unless I could get him out of that bunker.

"It's natural to look for answers," Dad continued. "To grasp at straws. Naturally, Meg wondered if Dr. Ballard knew something more than he'd said. Probably, Dr. Ballard wondered if Meg knew more than *she'd* said. So, when Meg found something that seemed to indicate maybe Dr. Ballard wasn't telling the truth, even though it had an innocent explanation, she naturally jumped to conclusions, and you jumped right along with her.

"But, Sam—riding in a car driven by an unlicensed, underaged driver? Following someone? Poking around that dangerous old bunker?" He shook his head. "I hope Meg is all right, but I'm glad at least you weren't in the car when she crashed. If it had happened down the road, at the bridge over the ravine, or if she'd lost control on the curve at Hunter Creek and hit the cliff . . ."

"She was a good driver," I said. "A safe driver."

His face clouded. "Obviously, she wasn't."

"She was running from Dr. Ballard!"

He took a deep breath, and now I realized the storm I had been fearing was already raging out of sight. "That's enough," he said, his voice several degrees colder than it had been a moment before. "Sam, I understand why you thought you had to do what you did, but it was stupid, wrong, and dangerous. You're grounded until further notice. Go upstairs. Take a shower—you're filthy—then go to your room, and don't come out until morning unless it's to go to the bathroom. No supper."

"Daddy—" I said, but then I stopped. No amount of pleading was going to move him. His mind was made up.

He got to his feet. "I'm going out to the crash site. See if I can help the search." He looked down at me, his face grim. "I'm trusting you to do what I tell you. But if you disobey me or try to get around this punishment . . . then I *won't* trust you next time. And once that trust is lost, it's very hard to get it back again. Do you understand?"

Feeling about two feet tall, I nodded.

"Good." He pointed to the stairs. "Go."

Tail metaphorically between my legs, I went.

CHAPTER 15
I HAVE UNWELCOME HOUSE GUESTS

In the shower, with hot water warming my chilled body and sluicing away the amazing amount of dirt I'd managed to pick up during the day's adventures, I felt both a little better and a lot worse. Better physically, worse in every other way.

Meg was missing. Dr. Ballard—Paracelsus—almost certainly had her. Lorenzo and the rest of the missing children were, I was certain, inside that underground bunker, now completely closed off. The landslide that I was convinced earth elementals had created would take days of work with heavy equipment to remove, and no one would make that effort because no one would believe me when I said I'd heard screaming from inside the now-buried bunker or seen Dr. Ballard come out of it.

I was grounded, and even if I hadn't been, there was nothing I could do. I couldn't dig away the landslide on my own. I couldn't help with the search. I couldn't do anything except stand there, naked and wet, and let my tears join the water coursing down my face.

But you can't stay in a shower all night. You certainly couldn't stay in *ours* all night, because after about ten minutes the water started to cool off, and then I had to hurry and get out because I knew from experience that once that happened, I only had a couple of minutes before it turned ice-cold.

I towelled off. I looked at myself in the mirror. I looked the same, except for the puffy red eyes. I was still Sam, I was still only thirteen years old, and I still felt helpless.

And then I felt the house shake.

My heart suddenly pounded. I went to the bathroom door, opened it, and stuck my head out into the hallway.

The house shook again, harder.

Did you ever see the original *Jurassic Park*? Shortly after they see ripples in a glass of water, the T-Rex arrives.

Something big was coming.

I ran into my bedroom and pulled on the same underwear, dirty shorts, and T-shirt I'd discarded on the floor fifteen minutes before—much as I would have preferred clean clothes, there wasn't time to dig them out. The house shook twice more before I was dressed. My shoes were down by the back door, so I left my feet bare. Then I turned off the bedroom light and cautiously pulled back the curtain so I could see out into the backyard.

The yard light was out. It hadn't been when I came home. It was hard to see much with only the stars giving light, but the yard looked . . . odd.

Then the house shook again, and I realized what I was seeing.

Something was walking toward the house, slow step by slow step.

Something vaguely man-shaped.

Something as tall as the barn.

Something as tall as my second-story window.

Starlight glistened off its wet surface as it moved. It was halfway to the house. Then it took another step, and it was two-thirds of the way to the house. I stared at it, frozen. *Earth elemental,* my mind told me, but this was *way* bigger than the one I had seen Lorenzo fight. *And "gnome" is* definitely *not the right word for it,* part of my brain rather hysterically noted.

Then it was almost to the house, and it raised an arm, and at the last second, I realized what was about to happen.

I turned and ran into the hall just before a mass of muddy earth and rotting leaves and broken twigs smashed through my bedroom window, right where I had been standing. It drew out again, leaving behind broken glass and plaster and wood, all smeared with foul-smelling muck. Gasping, I dashed for the stairs. *That thing could tear the whole house apart! I have to get out of here . . .*

I felt terrified but also angry—furious. *This is our house. That's my room!*

I heard another horrible crash. The thing must have reached into my room again, but by then, I was pounding down the stairs. I reached the hall, ran to the front door, yanked it open . . .

Crossing the road toward me was another terrifying figure, a woman shape made of water, not as tall as the earth elemental in the backyard but moving faster—a nymph.

I slammed the door shut, heart pounding.

I was trapped.

Or . . . maybe not.

I couldn't go out the back door: the mud-giant was out there. I couldn't go out the front door: the nymph was out there.

But there was one other way out of the house, our very *old* house, built when houses all had root cellars. The root cellar was separate from the house, but it served as a storm shelter, too, like the one in *The Wizard of Oz*, so it was connected to the basement with a short tunnel, just earth shored up with boards, with doors at both ends. I'd only ever been into the tunnel once—it was dirty and spidery and wormy, Dad had told me it wasn't safe and could collapse at any time, and anyway, it's not like we kept anything in the root cellar, Dad not being big on making preserves or pickles.

Dirt and spiderwebs—even actual spiders—suddenly didn't concern me in the slightest. And "could collapse at any time" sounded a lot safer than "giant man of mud tearing apart the house looking for me."

I ran to the door beneath the stairs, which led down to the basement. I yanked it open just as, at the far end of the hall, the back door and a big section of the wall came crashing in, propelled by a giant fist made of muck. I stared at the wreckage in horror, and then my head jerked the other way as the front door groaned and bent inward, water spouting around its edges. In a second, it would give way, and the nymph would see me . . .

I plunged down the basement stairs just as a final tearing, shattering crash spelled the end of our beautiful oak door. The basement door banged shut behind me.

Had the nymph spotted me?

I'd know in a minute. If she had, she'd be coming down into the basement after me. The terror of that thought drove me down the stairs two at a time so that I stumbled at the bottom and had to catch myself with a hand on the rough concrete of the foundation. I found the light switch by feel and flicked it on, bringing two bare incandescent bulbs to life.

Our basement had never been finished. The walls and

concrete floor had once been painted green, but little was left of that but flakes of colour here and there in the many, many cracks. The floor joists spanning the ceiling—just the underside of the first-story floorboards—hung maybe six inches above my head. Dad had to bend over whenever he went down there, except in one corner, where the floor was two feet lower to make room for the furnace.

The door leading into the tunnel to the root cellar was behind that furnace, and I picked my way to it between shelves that held an enormous collection of junk—most of it not even ours; when the previous owner had died, nobody had bothered to try to clean it out. Dad and I had rummaged through it many times, hoping for forgotten treasure, but the most interesting thing we'd ever found was the house's original blueprints, showing it had once had a water pump in the kitchen instead of a faucet and a coal furnace instead of a gas one . . .

I stopped just before stepping down beside the furnace. I didn't know how smart these elementals were, but they must have seen the root cellar door, and they just might figure it offered a third way out of the house beside the front and back. In which case, there might be something waiting for me out there.

But there was yet another way out: the old coal chute.

The chute itself was gone, but the opening in the wall was still there—just a metal door, not very big, but big enough for me to get through.

If I could reach it. I'd need something to stand on.

An old chair rested in one corner of the basement, just the seat, the back having broken off (last time we'd been down there together, Dad had joked that maybe it had been used in a bar fight). It was rickety and might fall apart if I wriggled it too much, but I only needed it for a second.

More crashing sounded upstairs. I felt sick about the damage to the house—I'd heard insurance didn't cover Acts of God, so would it cover Acts of Elementals?—but at least it sounded like the elementals were still looking for me up there, not down here.

I dragged the chair to the coal chute. Just as I stepped up onto the wooden seat, I heard the basement door open.

My heart, which hadn't exactly slowed since I first felt the house shake, suddenly raced even faster. I pushed as hard as I could at the rusty bolt securing the chute door.

It didn't budge. It felt like it and the door were cast out of one solid piece of iron.

Dad had a tool bench under the tiny windows in the corner under the stairs, the only part of the basement that got any light during the day. One of the bulbs hung over it, as well, so he could come down after dark and putter around.

I ran to the tool bench. Above me, the stairs creaked. I looked up and saw water seeping between the top step and the second one down. An icy drop fell onto my cheek. I gulped, grabbed a hammer, and ran back across the basement.

Halfway across, there was another crash, the house shuddered—and the lights went out, plunging me into darkness.

I bit off a scream. I found my way back to the coal chute by feel, got back up onto the old chair bottom, felt for the bolt, took a deep breath, and swung the hammer.

It hit solidly, with an enormous metallic crash that made my ears ring. If the nymph hadn't known for sure I was in the basement before, she would now. I imagined that water-woman slipping/flowing down the steps in the darkness behind me and swung the hammer again and again. The second time, I missed, but the third time, I connected and with a screech, the bolt gave way. The force of the blow drove the coal chute door upward just enough for me to catch a glimpse of starlit grass, and then it slammed shut again.

Behind me, the basement stairs creaked.

I pushed the swinging door open, jumped up, and scrambled through the opening, clambering out into the wet grass and weeds on my hands and bare knees. Then I straightened—

--and saw, right in front of me, the tree-trunk-sized legs of the earth elemental, so close that if it knew I was there, it could take a single step and crush me like a bug.

My breath caught in my throat. But then I heard the crash of something toppling in the basement and knew I had to move.

I looked up. The elemental, leaning forward like a man searching for something in the back of a cupboard, had its head close to the windows, swinging from side to side as it searched the second floor. I felt sick again at the thought of how badly damaged our house was, but at least it wasn't looking down at its feet.

I edged around to the right, toward the front of the house, keeping my back pressed to the shingles. Once I was around the corner, I turned to run, meaning to dash into the woods on the far side of the road—

—only to see a second woman-shaped mass of water standing in the middle of the road, watching the house.

The nymph saw me.

She came toward me.

I turned, thinking I could run past the feet of the earth

elemental, just in time to see the first nymph haul herself out of the basement through the coal chute.

And then, with a renewed sound of tearing wood and breaking glass, the earth elemental pulled back from the house, straightened—and looked right at me.

CHAPTER 16
I RUN AWAY FROM HOME

I was trapped, surrounded. I froze, but only for a second: then I ran toward the front of the house, thinking maybe I could dodge the nymph waiting there.

But she was faster than me and blocked my path, lifting her watery arms to grab me or strike me down, glowing red . . .

Wait a minute. Glowing red?

I barely had time to register that before she exploded. A huge gout of steam, a spray of hot water, and she was gone.

Lorenzo stood in her place, fire-Lorenzo, his flames brighter than ever, his body more defined than ever as if with each incarnation as an elemental, he was settling more firmly into the role . . . a scary thought. "Run!" he shouted at me, his voice roaring and crackling like a bonfire. "Into the woods across the road!"

I didn't have to be told twice. I dashed past him, so close his heat enveloped me for an instant like a warm—a *really* warm—hug, and across the street. I plunged in among the trees, only pausing to look back once I was deep in their shadows.

I saw the second nymph rush toward Lorenzo and saw her, too, explode into steam as she encountered him. Lorenzo's fire barely dimmed: a change from the first time I'd seen him face a nymph, out back of the barn, when he'd been extinguished—another sign his flames burned hotter than ever.

The giant earth elemental was slower to move and react, but now he roared, the first sound I had heard from him, and his massive fist came crashing down right where Lorenzo was—

But Lorenzo wasn't there anymore. Quicker than I could follow, quick as—well, as a flame—he flicked from where he had been standing to between the tree-trunk-sized legs of the earth elemental. He reached out his fiery arms and touched the elemental's knees. Then he blazed, brighter than I'd ever seen him. Brighter than I'd ever seen *any* fire.

And just like the nymphs, the earth elemental's legs exploded, this time in steam mixed with mud. Left literally without a leg to stand on, the elemental roared—and then, suddenly, was gone, leaving nothing behind but a towering mass of dirt that instantly collapsed . . .

. . . right where Lorenzo stood.

I screamed as his fire vanished beneath that thundering avalanche, then ran forward, branches tearing at my clothes. I burst back out onto the road and ran toward the pile of mud in the yard, shouting, "Lorenzo! *Lorenzo!*"

I felt a sudden touch of warmth behind me at the same moment that my shadow suddenly stretched out in front of me, wavering in flickering firelight. I skidded to a halt and spun around.

Lorenzo stood on the road by the damp spot that was all that was left of the first water elemental, a Greek statue of a boy made out of flame. "Lorenzo!" I reversed course and ran to him. I desperately wanted to hug him, but I couldn't even get close to him. "I thought you were gone!"

"I've learned to move fast in this form," he said, his voice no longer roaring like a bonfire but whispering and crackling like a yule log. "I flicked away just in time."

I turned and looked back at the house. The front door hung askew, and holes gaped in the upper story where my room's window used to be and down low where the nymph had smashed out after me through the coal chute door. I knew the back door had been smashed in, too, and didn't even want to think about what the inside of the house must look like, with water and mud everywhere. "Were they trying to kill me?" I said.

"I don't think so," Lorenzo said. "I think they were sent to kidnap you. Take you back to wherever my body is. Where the other kids are." He paused. "Where Meg is."

I stared at him. "Meg's there? You've seen her?"

"No," he said, "but I heard her. She yelled out, 'Lorenzo! I'm—' somewhere outside my room. Then her voice was cut off. Like someone had put a hand over her mouth. The nurse, or Paracelsus."

"We know who he is," I said.

He got very still. "Who?" he said.

"Dr. Ballard."

His fire blazed hotter. "What? Are you sure?"

I nodded. "And that's not all. I know where you are."

"How?"

I told him everything that had happened since the last time he'd seen us, how we'd followed Dr. Ballard to the bunker, how he'd made Meg's car crash and stolen her away, how he was out right now "helping" search for her.

"Dr. Ballard," Lorenzo said. He sounded angry but also sad. Or maybe disappointed. "I always liked him."

"I did, too." I looked at the house again. "Are those elementals dead?"

"I don't think so. I think they just lost form. Like when the nymph . . . put me out last time I was here." His flames shuddered. "That was awful. I threw up again when I got back to my own body." He turned his fiery gaze toward the pile of mud that had been the giant earth elemental. "If all that muck had landed on me, I don't know what would have happened. I'm glad I didn't find out."

I hated to ask the next question, but I had to. "Were the elementals here kids we knew?"

He shook his head. "No. They were very old. I could feel it. Very powerful, especially that giant earth elemental. And not really human anymore. No will of their own to speak of. Slaves of Paracelsus."

"You could feel all that?"

He nodded.

"Then . . ." My throat caught. "That's what he intends for you!"

"I think so," Lorenzo said, his voice little more than a whisper, like the hiss of sap from a log in the fire. Then it strengthened again. "But it's not going to work. I'm here against his will. He didn't send me. I came on my own."

"But how did you know I was in trouble?"

"I could feel it." Lorenzo reached out a hand toward me. I flinched and then hated myself for it as he drew it back again. *He wouldn't have touched me. He'd never hurt me.* "It's like there's a . . . a connection between us."

"A connection?"

His flame grew redder. For a second, I couldn't figure out why. Then it struck me. "Lorenzo? Are you *blushing*?"

He grew redder still and he looked at the ground, so all I could see of his head was a globe of swirling fire. "You'd think that would be one thing I wouldn't have to worry about while I look like this," he muttered.

My mouth dropped open. "Are you saying . . . this connection . . . you . . .?"

"I've had a crush on you since fourth grade," Lorenzo whisper-crackled.

My face suddenly felt as hot as he looked. "That's . . . I mean, we've always been . . . I mean, you're my best friend, but . . ." I stumbled to a halt.

He lifted his head. For about five seconds, we just stared at each other. This time, I looked away. "Well, I guess . . . that's a good thing." I gestured at the house. "All things considered."

"Yeah," Lorenzo said. Another silence. Then he added, "Um . . ."

"Yeah?"

"Have you . . . ever . . . you know . . . thought of me . . . like . . ."

I realized I didn't know how to answer that. Not without a lot of thought. Which would take a lot of time. Which we didn't have. "You're my best friend," I said firmly.

"Right," he said. "Friend."

Had his fire dimmed slightly? I hoped not. I cleared my throat. "Anyway, none of that matters now. The important question is, what do we do?" Inspiration struck. "I know," I said excitedly. "Come with me to the police. They can't deny their own eyes. When they see you, they'll know I'm telling the truth—"

But Lorenzo was shaking his head so hard sparks flew from it. "No! The only reason any of us are still alive is that Paracelsus . . . Dr. Ballard . . . doesn't think he's in any real danger. If the police came—even if we could convince them to come—he'd have an earth elemental collapse the whole bunker and crush us all. Then he'd vanish. Paracelsus is centuries old, Sam. He's made himself disappear before. He could . . ."

His voice faded, and his flame flickered like a candle in a gust of wind.

"Lorenzo?" I cried.

"He's coming," Lorenzo said, his voice fading till I could barely hear it. "I can feel him. His . . . his will. He's . . . he knows I'm out . . . that I'm not . . . he's . . ."

And then he disappeared with a soft pop, his warmth vanishing from my skin, cool air tugging at my hair as it rushed back into the space his flame had filled.

"Lorenzo!" I cried, but the only sound I heard was the whisper of wind through the trees . . .

. . . and faint, but growing closer, the sound of sirens.

Maybe someone had heard the house being broken apart; maybe someone had glimpsed a flicker of Lorenzo's flame from one of the houses higher up in the valley. However it had happened, someone had realized something strange was going on and had called the cops.

And I couldn't stay to talk to them. Lorenzo was right. If Dr. Ballard—Paracelsus—felt really threatened, he'd cut his losses and vanish, leaving no one behind to talk. Not Lorenzo, not the other kids from my class, not Meg . . .

. . . not me.

Lorenzo had said he'd felt Paracelsus's will forcing him back into his body. What if the next time Paracelsus sent elementals after me, he made sure Lorenzo couldn't come to help? Without Lorenzo, I wouldn't have escaped *these* elementals.

I had to run, hide. I couldn't be found by the police, by *anyone*.

I ran back to the house, past the hole in the wall where the coal chute had been, back around to the back porch, a shattered shamble of broken wood and scattered shingles. The lights in the house had gone out, but my eyes had adjusted to the starlight, and I spotted the corner of my backpack, never unpacked since we'd returned from that awful camping trip, peeking out from under the smashed-in door.

I tugged at it. It wouldn't budge.

The siren wailed, closer and closer. The cops would be there any second!

I pulled with all my strength. Something gave way, and the backpack came loose so abruptly that I fell hard onto my rear end.

I scrambled up, holding the pack by one strap, and ran for the woods, out past the barn, right where I had seen Lorenzo for the first time. I had just made it in among the trees, the damp leaves cold around my still-bare feet, when the sirens swelled, and two cop cars rounded the corner, their headlights flashing over the ruined side of the house. I faded away into the shadows, hearing the banging of car doors and the shouts of the cops as I slipped through the trees.

I felt horrible about the damage to the house.

I felt even worse when I thought of Dad coming home to a wrecked house and a missing daughter. I had promised him I wouldn't go anywhere, that I'd stay put, but I couldn't keep that promise. Not only was it not safe for me, it wasn't safe for *him*. What if he'd been there when the elementals attacked? They might just want to grab me and take me back to Paracelsus's bunker, but they would never have left a witness. Dad would have . . .

My breath caught in my throat.

Dad would have died. Like Mom.

Better he think *I* was dead than *that*. After all, if I succeeded, if I really managed to rescue Lorenzo and the others, I'd eventually be home safe and sound. He could ground me until I went to college if he wanted to. Right then, with branches trying to tear my clothes and scratching my bare legs, with my equally bare feet cold and bruised, without a plan, without a friend, five years locked in my room sounded like heaven.

But heaven could wait.

Meg and Lorenzo needed me.

I wouldn't let them down.

Cold, tired, filthy, and aching, I ran away from home.

CHAPTER 17
I TAKE A HIKE

Have you ever tried to run through the forest? Even in the daytime, it's not easy. There are too many branches, too many roots, too many rocks and fallen logs and gullies and streams. At night, it's even worse. So yes, I ran, but not for very long because after about a minute I stubbed my bare big toe and tripped and went sprawling and scraped my knee and got a mouthful of musty leaves.

After that, I picked my way more carefully. But I kept moving, while behind me, I heard shouts and the crackle of radio chatter; kept moving until I couldn't hear any of that anymore, and then kept moving even longer. I wasn't lost, exactly—there were stars in the sky, and I could look up and see I was heading more or less in the direction I wanted to be heading, back toward the bunker where Lorenzo and Meg and the other missing children were prisoners.

Not that there was any chance I could get there overnight. I already felt exhausted after everything that had happened. I had to rest, at least for a few hours. I could start moving at first light. I figured it would take me most of the next day on foot, especially since I'd have to avoid people and buildings. My goal right then was just to get far enough away from our house so that neither the cops nor any other elementals Paracelsus might send after me could find me.

For a while, adrenaline kept me wide awake and moving, but as it faded, so did my energy, draining away from me like water going down the drain until I couldn't take one more step.

I had a little fold-up tent in the backpack and a lightweight sleeping bag. Better yet, I discovered I still had a pair of flip-flops tucked away in there that I'd forgotten about, wrapped up in a swimsuit, which was wrapped up in a towel. I hadn't gone swimming in the nearby lake when we'd gone camping because I was already wet enough, thanks to the rain. Flip-flops aren't exactly good hiking shoes, but they were better than bare feet.

My backpack also held a battery-operated camp lantern, but there was no way I was going to turn it on, not when I was trying not to be seen by anyone. I did risk using the little LED flashlight hanging on the outside of the backpack, but I held it cupped in my hand so that the light just seeped out between my fingers, dim and pink but better than nothing. I set up my tent, unrolled the sleeping bag, climbed inside its blessed warmth, and curled up, and remembered as I lay there, both more tired and more awake than I had ever been in my life, how the last time I had slept in that tent and sleeping bag had been the night I had seen Lorenzo's face in the fire.

And now Lorenzo was *all* fire, and if I didn't do something, he might never be a boy again.

And he has a crush on me.

I hugged myself, lying there in the sleeping bag. I'd

thought about boys and maybe having a boyfriend in a vague sort of that-might-be-nice-someday way, but I'd never thought of Lorenzo as my boyfriend. He was just my friend, who happened to be a boy. It was a little weird, knowing instead of just thinking about girls in general like most boys did, he'd been thinking about one girl in particular—and that girl was *me*. But if he *hadn't* felt that way about me, he might not have had the connection with me that had enabled him to find me and tell me what was going on.

It made me that much more determined to do everything I could to save him.

If I could.

Paracelsus had had his earth elementals seal the garage entrance to the bunker with a landslide. How would I get inside?

I puzzled over it as I lay there, but not for long because I was so tired I couldn't keep my eyes open. Sleep had almost claimed me when a thought hit me, and my eyes flew open again, not that that changed what I could see inside the pitch-black tent.

Even gopher holes have back doors.

A bunker with only one way out would be a death trap, in the event of a fire or a fall-in . . . or a raid by government agents, which was more likely what the survivalists who had built the place had been afraid of. The bunker *had* to have a back door, probably a secret one. And although Dr. Ballard—Paracelsus—could have his elementals uncover the main entrance as easily as he'd had them cover it, why would he? After seeing the apparently years-old landslide burying the front doors, the police had completely discounted my story. Why would he disturb that perfect camouflage?

He wouldn't—he'd use the back door. Which meant I could use it, too.

Assuming I could find it.

I lay awake for a few more minutes, but not very many. Sleep came creeping back, and this time, it got me.

I woke to birdsong, grey light, and a crick in my neck. One thing I hadn't had in my backpack was a pillow.

With a groan, I sat up. The inside of my mouth felt fuzzy, and I had that icky feeling you always have when you sleep all night in your clothes—especially dirty ones like mine—but at least no one had found me while I slept. I sat up inside the sleeping bag, unzipped the tent flap, leaned my head through it, and took a look around.

I'd ended up in a little hollow in the mountain slope. Fir trees rose around me, mist slithering around their trunks like cold white snakes. Chilly air nipped my nose. I hated to leave the warm cocoon of my sleeping bag, but the sooner I got moving, the sooner I'd get to the compound.

I wriggled back to sit fully inside the tent, keeping the sleeping bag around me while I drank one of the four bottles of water the backpack had contained and ate one of the five granola bars that were all the food I had. Then I sighed, got out of the sleeping bag, rolled it up, folded the tent, packed everything into my backpack except the flip-flops (which I put on), shouldered the pack, and set out through the woods.

I couldn't get lost, not really, not with the mountains to my left and the valley to my right. As the morning wore on, I had to skirt an acreage with a big log house in the centre. It had the look of a summer place, and no smoke rose from its chimney, but I made sure to stay out of sight anyway.

I hadn't gone much farther when I came to a road of sorts, just a rutted gravel track through the woods. I looked both ways as carefully as I'd learned to do when I was seven and walking to school on my own for the first time, then darted across like a frightened squirrel—the same way I used to cross roads back then—and hurried on through the trees.

The next road I came to was both paved and busier: it went up over the ridge of our valley and down into the next one over. I heard the sound of traffic on it long before I saw flashes of coloured metal and glass between the trees.

Still, near a small town like Limberpine, even the busiest road isn't very busy. My path took me to a straight stretch between two curves, one a hundred yards to my right and one about twice that far to my left. I hesitated. If someone came around either of those curves as I crossed the road, they might see me before I could get into the woods on the other side. But I had to take the chance.

Sure enough, halfway across the road, I heard a car coming. I was off the road when the car rounded the corner to my right, coming from the direction of the town, but that's when I found the fence I hadn't been able to see from the other side—the *barbed-wire* fence. I was still trying to get over it without hurting myself when the car zipped past. I shot it a quick glance.

Not just a car—a *police* car.

That got me up and over the fence. I crouched in among the trees on the far side of the fence, sucking my scratched thumb, bleeding from a much longer scratch in my right leg —and staring at the flip-flop that had come off my foot as I'd scrambled over the fence and now lay on the other side, in plain sight to me, at least, though I couldn't tell if it was visible to the . . .

The cop car reappeared, rolling slowly back down the road in the other direction. I said a word that Dad would have grounded me for if he'd heard it, then flattened myself belly-down on the damp ground, peering out through the tall weeds. I didn't dare try to run—the movement would catch the cops' eyes for sure. Instead, I just lay there and waited and hoped they wouldn't see the errant flip-flop.

The driver's door opened, and a cop got out. Then the other door opened, and another cop got out. They were the same ones who had driven me home the night before.

". . . didn't see anything . . ." the driver-cop said. I could only catch the occasional word when the wind blew it my way.

". . . thought I did . . . could've . . . girl . . ." replied the passenger-side cop, who, of course, would have been the one looking out the window.

They were looking for me. Or Meg. Or both. I said a different and even worse bad word under my breath.

". . . take a look . . ."

". . . nothing there now . . . must have seen us . . . hide?"

". . . colour . . . see?"

"White . . ."

". . . Sam . . . white T-shirt . . ."

Now, bad words were running on a constant loop inside my head.

The driver reached inside the car and pulled out a pair of binoculars. He scanned my side of the road, and I shoved my head down to the ground and hoped the weeds and bushes and shadows would be enough to hide both me and my fallen footwear on the fence's far side.

After roughly forever, I heard the driver's voice again.

". . . don't see anything . . ."

". . . could have . . . a bird . . ."

". . . report it . . . searchers . . ."

One door slammed, then the other. I heard the car start up and the crunch of its tires as it backed up, turned around, and drove off up the road in the direction it had been travelling originally, but I waited another five minutes before I dared look up.

They were gone. A second later, so was I, dashing forward to grab the flip-flop, shoving it on my foot, and then running into the woods as fast as I could run in flip-flops. I stopped when the road was out of sight behind me, but my heart pounded for several more minutes.

It sounded like the one cop had seen a flash of white from my T-shirt, but no more than that. They knew Meg had been wearing red, so they didn't figure it was her—but they knew I was wearing white, so they weren't so sure it wasn't me. They would have already radioed it in. A search party might be here soon—maybe *really* soon, if it wasn't far away. Maybe even with dogs. I had to keep moving.

Five minutes later, I came across a farm, as I should have guessed I would from the barbed-wire fence. The fence clearly wasn't meant to keep livestock in—as far as I could tell from the varied rows of plants in the field I'd stumbled on, the farm grew various kinds of vegetables—but to keep deer out. The windows of the white-shingled farmhouse stared at me from beneath the frowning line of the dark-green roof as I hurried around the edge of the field. My stomach growled, and I thought about pulling a Peter Rabbit and stealing a few carrots, but I couldn't be sure my own "Farmer McGregor" wouldn't be watching. Instead, around noon, with the farm far behind, I ate two more granola bars and drank more of my bottled water.

For the rest of the afternoon, I toiled through forest I might have thought no one had ever walked through before if not for the massive tree stumps I kept having to skirt. Clearly, the original growth had been cut down for lumber, and the current woods were second-growth, the trees, though they towered high overhead, mere saplings compared to the original giants.

When Dr. Ballard—Paracelsus—was young, this tree was still here, I thought as I scrambled over a stump so big that if I'd laid down on it, I could have stretched out my arms and legs and not found the edges with my fingers or toes.

Not that he had been anywhere near here then. He would have been in Europe.

I wondered how long ago he had come to North America. And then I wondered how many children he had stolen over the years, how many kids he had ripped from their parents and brothers and sisters, how many he had imprisoned in dark places and transformed into elementals.

He's a monster. As big a monster as Jack the Ripper or Hitler. Do you really think you can bring him down?

It was a chilling thought, but I just let myself be chilled and kept walking through the trees. Lorenzo and Meg were depending on me. The other kids didn't know I was coming, but they needed my help just as much. If I could sneak inside while Dr. Ballard was out, maybe I could free them all before he came back. The teams searching for Meg and me couldn't be too far away. Once they saw the kids and the kids told their stories, they'd have to believe me. They'd arrest Dr. Ballard. He'd never do this to any other children ever again . . .

Then I shook my head. How could you keep someone like that in prison? An earth elemental would make short work of any jail ever built. He'd simply vanish, establish another new identity, wait his chance to kidnap another group of children . . .

Why? I wondered then. *Why does he keep needing new elementals? Do they wear out? Does he do it just because he can?*

Or is there some other reason?

What if he needed the kids for something else? What if only some of them could be made into elementals?

What else do kids have that he doesn't have?

And then it struck me, so suddenly and horribly I stumbled and brought up short, one hand against a spruce tree's trunk.

Youth.

Paracelsus was centuries old. He'd discovered the secret to eternal youth, the Philosopher's Stone, or he couldn't still be alive. What if, when he kidnapped kids, he only turned *some* of them into elementals? What if he used the rest to provide him with new life, sucking the youth out of them to keep himself young, to stretch out his long existence?

It made horrible, sickening sense. Dr. Ballard, who used to be my favourite teacher, wasn't just an alchemist, he was a *vampire.*

I pushed against the spruce trunk to straighten myself up and strode forward with new determination. *Well, then,* I thought with all the bravado I could muster, which I admit wasn't much, *it's high time someone drove a stake into his heart.*

Two hours later, with the sun hanging low over the western mountains, stretching the shadows of the trees across the forest floor like long, dark fingers, I came across a high chain-link fence topped with curly barbed wire. I recognized it instantly as the fence around the bunker's compound.

I stared up at the barbed wire, then both ways along the fence.

Now, all I had to do was get in.

CHAPTER 18
I SNEAK IN THE BACK DOOR

There comes a time in every girl's life when she really wishes she'd thought to pack wire cutters.

I looked left. Unbroken chain-link fence.

I looked right. Ditto—although somewhere down that way, around the corner and along the next stretch of fence, was the gate Meg and I had driven through. Using it seemed risky, though, even if the cops had left it open and not padlocked it shut since last night. There would still be searchers in the woods, and they were more likely to be down there, closer to where the car had crashed.

To my left, the fence had to eventually run into the rising slope of the mountain, although I couldn't see far enough through the forest to be sure. Thinking that might offer me a way over or through, I set off in that direction.

The fence remained depressingly unbroken. The trees grew close to it, but being spindly spruce and fir, they didn't do me the courtesy of extending long, easily accessible branches over the barbed wire. All I could do was work my way along the chain link and hope that somewhere, somehow, there was another way through.

The fence turned right, just where the slope steepened. In fact, the slope rose so close to the fence that I found it much harder to follow it—but it still didn't offer any way through or over.

Until, suddenly, it did.

When I was little, Dad used to joke about the WATCH FOR FALLING ROCKS signs we'd see as we drove. "Heads up!" he'd say. "Get out the steel umbrella!" (Dad jokes are the worst jokes.) But in the mountains, falling rock really is a thing and some time or other, one the size of a large St. Bernard (or a small refrigerator) had come bounding down the mountainside and slammed into the fence. It hadn't gone through, but it had pushed one of the posts over at a forty-five-degree angle.

That gave me my way in. I took off my backpack, scrambled up on the boulder, threw my backpack over the fence into the compound, and then jumped, barely clearing the spiralling barbed wire atop the fence before I hit the ground, tumbling over and over a few times. Breathless, bruised, and barefoot again (the flip-flops had both come off when I jumped and now lay outside the fence), bleeding because the long scratch on my leg from my earlier barbed-wire encounter had re-opened and even dirtier than before—which I wouldn't have thought possible—I got up, brushed grass and soil off my knees and shorts and T-shirt, shouldered my backpack, and finally looked around for some sign of the back door I'd convinced myself had to exist.

I saw no sign of the bunker at all—especially since the sun had now slipped below the western mountains, casting everything in shadow, even though true sunset was still a couple of hours away.

Think, I told myself. *It's underground. It's got to get air. There must be air vents. If I were going to build a back door, I'd put it close to the vents so I only had to dig one hole.*

So, I started looking for air vents, even though I didn't have a clue what they'd look like. They could be disguised as rocks or tree stumps or squirrels, for all I knew.

Okay, probably not squirrels.

Then, of course, I promptly *saw* some squirrels, but since they scampered away, climbed a tree, and chattered angrily at me, I felt confident they weren't really a disguised ventilation system.

I saw lots of rocks. They were just rocks.

I saw lots of tree stumps. They were just tree stumps.

When I finally did find an air vent, close to where the ground sloped up to what I guessed was the ridge beneath which the now-buried garage doors had been set, I was almost disappointed. Bushes and weeds had hidden it from me, but it wasn't disguised at all: it was a big, bent-forward tube like you see on the decks of ships, set on a concrete platform about six inches tall. A metal screen covered the end of the tube. I bent close, put my ear to it, and listened.

I couldn't hear anything except the sound of a fan. A breeze tugged my hair toward the tube, which meant air was being sucked into the underground compound, which meant there was a direct connection between the vent and where I wanted to get to—but the tube was too small for me to fit through even if I took off the screen, and even if it hadn't been, dropping down into the blades of a fan didn't appeal to me.

I straightened and stared around, looking for the entrance

I was *sure* had to be there. But all I saw were more rocks and trees. I thought for a second, then started circling around the vent, spiralling out from it, wider and wider.

I never did *see* the back door—instead, I tripped over it. As I shuffled my bare feet through a drift of old leaves, I caught my toes on something so hard I fell forward, my knees and hands banging down on something metal with a sound like a booming drum.

A trap door!

I scrambled to my feet and ran as fast as I could to a nearby stand of bushes, crouching behind them and freezing there like a startled rabbit, waiting to see if my noisy discovery of the door brought someone to investigate. Five minutes passed. No one popped out of the door like a Jack-in-the-box, so I took a deep breath, got up, returned to the door, knelt down, and pushed the leaves away.

I expected something small and square, but what I uncovered was a regular-sized door, set flat in the ground—kind of like our own storm cellar door. A handle stuck up. I tugged at it, expecting the door to be locked . . . but it lifted easily, although with a horrible grinding sound. It was a lot heavier than I expected: I had to use both hands to heave it all the way up, then had to let it go. It slammed against the concrete frame with an even bigger crash than I'd made when I landed on the door on my hands and knees, and I ran back to the bushes again because if anyone was down there, surely they'd heard *that*.

But nobody came running up the concrete steps the door had revealed or popped out firing a machine gun or threw a grenade or released a pack of killer dogs, all things that *could* have happened—at least, based on TV and movies, which were proving to be less educational about these matters than one might have hoped.

I finally returned to the door, knelt to look down the stairs it had revealed—and heard a sound, distant, faint, but unmistakable: a child, crying. That decided me. After a moment's thought, I took my little pocket-sized LED flashlight out of my backpack, then took off the pack itself and hid it behind the same bush I'd hidden all of myself behind a moment before, piling some leaves on it to be sure it couldn't be spotted from the door. Then, I flicked on the flashlight and started down the metal stairs, ice-cold beneath my bare feet.

Enough of the fast-fading light outside spilled down the stairs to show me the way to the first landing, maybe fifteen feet down. There, a dim bulb inside a rusty metal cage revealed the way down another stretch of stairs, past a second light. Another light burned—barely—at the next landing, where the steps turned left again. I kept the flashlight in my hand anyway. It wasn't big enough to hit anybody with, but I could shine it in their eyes and then run.

With every step I took, the crying grew louder, sobs filled with so much hopelessness and fear my own throat closed in sympathy. I wanted to run down the stairs to help, but I held myself back. After all, just because no one had come running to the door didn't mean they weren't down there, waiting to grab me when I finally appeared.

It belatedly occurred to me, as I turned the second landing, that I should have closed the door behind me once I was inside: if Dr. Ballard or the mysterious nurse were out and came back, they'd know at once someone had found the door and gone into the bunker. But as I continued to creep down, step by silent step (my bare feet, cold though they were, at least gave me the advantage of stealth), I realized that closing the door wouldn't have hidden my tracks anyway because I couldn't pull the leaves back over the door from this side.

A few steps later, I realized the fact there had been leaves covering the door was a *good* sign since they would have had to be put there by someone leaving, not someone arriving. By then, I was at the bottom of the third flight of stairs and there was no way I was going back up, so I was glad I had reasoned my way out of it. The door was so heavy I might not have been able to close it from the inside anyway.

That third and final flight ended in a door propped open with a rock. Beyond it stretched a short hallway lit by a single incandescent bulb. At the end was another propped-open door. It had once had a glass window in it, but only a few jagged shards remained in the frame. All I could see beyond the door was a bare, blank wall, but through the opening still came the sound of sobbing.

The hairs rose on the back of my neck, and my hand tightened on the flashlight, but I kept going. No matter what horrors I might find, I had to. I was the only person except for Dr. Ballard and the mysterious nurse who knew where the missing kids were. If I ran back and tried to find the searchers in the woods, I might run into Dr. Ballard—or he might realize what was going on and summon his elementals to collapse the bunker, killing everyone. *No one would believe me anyway*, I thought. *They'd haul me back to town again, Dad would lock me up until I'm thirty-five, and Dr. Ballard would keep on doing whatever it is he's doing.*

And so, even though it was the hardest thing I'd ever done, I took a step toward that door, and then another, and then another . . . and then I was opening it, and then I was in the space beyond.

A dimly lit corridor stretched to my left and right. To the

left, it ended after a short distance in a rust-red door marked HEATING AND VENTILATION. There wouldn't be any kids in there.

To the right, the corridor went a little farther to a T-intersection. I walked down to it, past more of the dim, metal-caged bulbs. Only about half of them still worked. It all seemed strangely familiar, and I suddenly realized why: it looked a lot like a particularly scary level in a computer game I'd played once, one of those zombies-are-everywhere things-jumping-out-at-you splattered-with-gore computer games—one which had given me nightmares for about a week.

Oh, thanks for digging that up, brain, I thought to myself. *You're a real pal.*

My brain did not defend itself, instead maintaining a sullen, or possibly terrified, silence.

I slowed as I came to the intersection and cautiously looked both ways.

Much like in that computer game I wished I hadn't remembered, I still didn't have a choice of which way to go. To the right, the corridor ended after maybe twenty feet in a pile of twisted concrete and steel rods and earth. Either there'd been an earthquake, or Dr. Ballard's earth elementals had been at work.

I wondered what had been down that way that Dr. Ballard had wanted buried and felt cold all over again. This bunker had been abandoned by its creators half a century ago. Had he used it before? Were the bones of other lost children beneath that rubble?

With a shudder, I turned the other way.

In that direction, the corridor stretched about twenty feet to the top of a staircase. The closer I came to those stairs, the louder the sobbing became. Trailing my hand on the cold metal railing, I descended the stairs, emerging into the middle of one wall of a big square chamber with doors all around it.

Only four of the bulbs in the twenty-or-so metal upside-down-bowl-shaped fixtures hanging on chains from the ceiling were working, casting pools of light over a bunch of old-fashioned chrome-framed green-vinyl chairs, mostly overturned, surrounding circular, green-topped, chrome-rimmed tables. Opposite me were two closed doors. To my right were two more. One stood open, revealing nothing but darkness; the other was closed, but yellow light glowed through its little square window.

Shining my flashlight to the left, I saw a long counter and could just make out the stainless-steel fixtures of a big kitchen behind it. On the counter stood a pile of plates, a collection of cutlery, and what looked like bags of potato chips and loaves of bread. I hoped that meant the kids were being fed, at least.

But then my nose wrinkled because the smell of the place was enough to make anyone lose their appetite. It was an awful mixture of rotting muck—the smell of the earth elemental—and outhouse and boys' locker room (yes, I've been in a boys' locker room; I know what they smell like). Whatever this place had been once, now it was just a horrible, nasty prison.

And the prisoners were my friends.

CHAPTER 19
I FIND OUT I WAS RIGHT THE FIRST TIME

For a moment, I wished I'd never left home, wished I'd waited for the police instead of running away after the elementals attacked, wished Lorenzo had never shown up in our campfire, wished Dad and I had left town after Mom died and never looked back and I'd never *been* in Dr. Ballard's Grade 7 science class . . .

But I *was* there. Meg was there. Lorenzo was there. Other kids I'd gone to school with all my life were there.

The sobbing had never stopped. It came from behind the closed door to the right with the glowing window in it. Turning off my flashlight and sticking it in my pocket—I felt horribly conspicuous with it on—I approached the door cautiously.

At least, I *thought* I was being cautious. Trouble was, in the dark, I banged into one of the chairs, toppling it. It hit the floor with a crash before I could catch it.

My heart leaped into my throat and I stood stock still, quivering, waiting for more lights to come on, someone to shout, someone to come bursting into the room . . .

But none of that happened. Instead, a quavering voice came from the room in front of me, where the sobbing had cut off abruptly with the crash of the chair. "Who's there?"

I didn't recognize the voice right away. But I recognized the fear in it, and that was enough to unfreeze my legs.

Reaching the door, I peered through its window into the room beyond.

Lorenzo had described the room he was being kept in as a kind of dorm room, with a desk and its own bathroom. This one had a bathroom—I could see into it through an open door across from the one I stood at—but it definitely wasn't a dorm room. It was dominated by, of all things, a pool table, shoved up against the wall to my right, with more of the green-vinyl chairs piled on top of it.

It did have the ugly brown carpet and puke-green walls Lorenzo had described. Apparently, the survivalists had had a really lousy interior decorator.

Closer to the door, I could see the end of a cot, and two bare legs and two bare feet.

On my side of the door was a simple sliding bolt. I drew it, took a deep breath, wished I hadn't as the dank stink of the old bunker filled my mouth and nose, opened the door, and stepped inside.

The bare legs and feet I had seen belonged to a girl in a thin blue hospital gown, sitting up on the cot, which was covered with a military-looking green blanket. Blue eyes, red-rimmed from weeping, stared at me from a wan, blotchy, hollow-cheeked face, framed by tangled blonde hair. "Sam?" the girl whispered. "Sam? Is that really you?"

I stared at her, horrified. The girl in the cot was Melanie Fillion, the girl whose locket Dr. Ballard had had in his pocket, whose jacket he had had in the trunk of his car;

Melanie, the prettiest girl in Grade 7, with long blonde hair and perfect skin; Melanie, who could sing and dance and whose frequent smiles and laughs lit up the whole class-room. Now here she was, locked in a room, pale, sickly, almost emaciated. Maybe they were feeding the kids, but clearly, they weren't feeding them very well. I felt horror, then pity . . . and then, anger. More anger than I'd ever felt before.

"Sam?" Melanie repeated, from the sound of her voice on the verge of tears again. "Say something. Are you really here? Or am I seeing things?"

"I'm really here," I said. I looked took a quick look out the window to make sure there was no one in the big dining room, then stepped closer to her. "Is everyone here? The whole class?"

"I don't know for sure," Melanie said. "We eat together, out there in the big room, but I haven't seen everyone." Her voice fell a little. "Sam, I'm sorry, but . . . I haven't seen Lorenzo."

"He's all right," I said. *Well, except for being turned into an elemental*, I thought. But I didn't want to explain all that just now. I took another look at Melanie. "But are *you* all right? You look so . . . thin. They must not be feeding you very much."

"Not much," Melanie said. "But even what they give us I can't eat. I'm never hungry." Her voice fell to a whisper. "*He* comes in here sometimes. A man wearing a mask. He just sits and . . . and looks at me. He looks at me, and I get dizzy, and I fall asleep. And then I wake up, and he's gone, and I feel so weak. I feel weak all the time now." Her lip trembled, and it obviously took her a lot of effort to keep from sobbing again.

"You don't . . . leave your body?"

She gave me a bewildered look. "What? No, I just fall asleep."

I felt ill. This was the other side of what Dr. Ballard was doing. Lorenzo, maybe one or two others, he was trying to turn into elementals, but the rest of the kids, he was sucking the life out of to keep himself young. How long could that go on before he killed somebody?

"I can't believe I've always liked him," I muttered.

Melanie still looked bewildered. "Who?"

"Who?" I stared at her. "Dr. Ballard!" I made his name sound like a curse word. "He's behind all of this!"

"No," she said, shaking her head. "You're wrong. He's the one who feeds us. He even tries to cheer us up. He's brought us games. Even books. He keeps telling us our families are all okay, and we'll see them again soon." Her voice dropped to a whisper. "But none of us believe him."

It was my turn to blink. "But then, the masked man who comes in here—"

"It's not Dr. Ballard," Melanie said. "It's the vice-principal. It's Mr. Reiniger."

I felt a bit like the ground had just shifted under my feet. "You're sure? I mean, the mask . . ."

"Yes, I'm sure," she said, sounding a little miffed. "I've heard him talking. I recognize his accent."

I'm not too proud to admit that my first reaction was, *Hey, I was right after all!* But then I thought, *If Reiniger is Paracelsus, why is Dr. Ballard involved at all?*

Maybe it made me hate him a little less, knowing he was at least making sure his Grade 7 science class got food, but only a little, because he was clearly in cahoots with Reiniger and the woman Lorenzo had mentioned—presumably Mrs. Reiniger, his "deathly ill" wife.

So, to recap, our vice-principal was really Paracelsus, who was trying to turn some kids, including Lorenzo, into soulless enslaved elemental monsters and sucking the life right out of other kids in order to live forever, and our science teacher, Dr. Ballard, had not only helped him kidnap the entire Grade 7 science class, he was doing his best in the outside world to deflect all suspicion from Paracelsus and himself and ensure the authorities had no clue where the kids had gone.

But, hey, at least he was making them sandwiches.

Exactly when had my life turned into a straight-to-video horror movie?

Something else had been bothering me. "Where are your clothes?" I said. "Why are you wearing a hospital gown?"

"It's all they let us wear," she said. "Hospital gowns for the girls, just pyjama bottoms for the boys, not even shirts. They took away our own clothes and shoes as soon as we got here. They said it's so we won't run away. And to make laundry easier." She sniffed at her sleeve. "Dr. Ballard takes them away to wash. But only once a week, and sometimes not even that often. And while he's doing the wash, we just have to sit here in a blanket."

That explained some of the smell. I pulled myself together and turned to the door. "Well," I said. "I'm here now. All I have to do is find the others and . . ."

My voice trailed off. A door had just opened somewhere out in the common room.

It's okay, I thought, as best I could over the sudden pounding of my heart in my ears. *Whoever it is, Reiniger, Dr. Ballard, or the woman—if they come in here, I'll surprise them, knock them down, get past them, escape, get help . . .*

That was as much of a plan as I could come up with, and it wasn't much of a plan, since it skipped over several over several important details, like how I, a skinny thirteen-year-old girl, was going to overpower a grown man or woman.

Footsteps approached the room. I abandoned my James Bondish scheme, whispered, "Stay quiet!" to Melanie, and the hid the only place there was to hide: the bathroom.

Dark and damp, that bathroom had trapped more than its share of the general miasma of rot and decay that clung to everything in the bunker, and contributed to it, too. It looked like it hadn't been cleaned since the survivalists left decades ago.

The door opened and closed again. I heard a voice, a woman's voice, with an accent . . . not German, though. French, maybe? "'Ave you seen anyone?" the voice snapped. "A strange-air?" (Well, that's what it sounded like.)

"No," Melanie said. "How could I see anyone in here?"

"You are lying," the woman said. "Your door, it has been unbolted. From the outside."

I wanted to jump out right then, but I didn't dare. The woman had to be bigger and stronger than me. For all I knew, she had a gun.

Just wait. She'll open the door again. That's when I'll rush it out. She'll have her back to me. I can knock her down, get past he . . .

And then what? a part of me asked, kind of snarkily, I thought.

Escape the bunker. Get into the woods. Get to town before they can chase you down. Tell the police. Convince them I'm not crazy. Get help. Get everyone rescued . . .

Gee, the snarky part of me replied. *Is that all? Back to being James Bond, are we?*

The door opened. She was leaving. I had to go *now*.

I threw open the bathroom door, rushed into the room . . .

. . . and stopped dead, because the door hadn't opened to let the woman leave.

It had opened to let someone else through.

"Sam," said a German-accented voice from behind a hockey mask. "So nice of you to join us."

CHAPTER 20
I AM BESIDE MYSELF

My first thought was, *Melanie's right, that's Mr. Reiniger.* My second thought was, *How did he know I was in here?* My third thought was, *What's that in his hand?*

There was no fourth thought, because the thing in his hand was a hypodermic, and before I could react, he had stepped forward, grabbed my wrist, and stabbed me in the shoulder with it—which hurt a lot, but only for a second, because right after that, everything went black.

I DIDN'T WAKE up all at once. I woke up a little at a time, struggling to consciousness as though I were fighting my way to the surface of a muddy pond—not that I've ever done that, but it felt the way I imagine it would feel, right down to the having a bad taste in my mouth when I was finally completely awake.

I noticed a couple of other things, too, neither of which made me feel good.

First, someone had taken my clothes off me and put me in a blue hospital gown, just like Melanie had been wearing. With just that thin piece of cloth to cover me, I was freezing cold.

Second, I was in a cot just like Melanie's—only, unlike her, I was strapped down by two leather belts, one across my chest, one across my legs below my knees. I struggled for a few seconds, but it was hopeless. I gave up and peered around the room instead.

This one was smaller than Melanie's repurposed rec room. It looked like it must have once been an office: there was an old desk pushed up against the wall at the foot of the bed, a filing cabinet in the corner, and a wooden swivel chair overturned on the ugly brown carpet. (I guess even survivalist cults have paperwork.) There was no bathroom, which might be a problem eventually but wasn't right now.

I started feeling sorry for myself. Why had I come here? I could have begged Dad to take me out of town as soon as the police drove me home. We could have gone to the Last Splash waterpark in Calgary we last visited when I was eleven. We could have gone to see Grandma in her nursing home in Victoria. We could have gone to Regina to see the Mountie museum. We could have . . .

We could have. But we hadn't. And if we had, if I'd somehow convinced Dad to do any of those things, I would have been abandoning Meg and Lorenzo and all the other kids imprisoned down here.

Great, I told myself. *You wanted to be a hero. So instead of abandoning them, you joined them.* I pushed my body fruitlessly against the straps for a second, then fell back again. *Some hero.*

And then I heard voices, a man's and a woman's, coming my way. I closed my eyes and let my head flop to one side. I tried to breathe slowly and shallowly. Let them think I was still asleep. They couldn't do anything bad to me until I was awake, could they?

" . . . Ballard has led them on a wild-goose chase." I recognized Vice-Principal Reiniger's thick German accent again. "He has been most useful."

"*Oui*, as you knew he would be," said the woman. "It was most clever of you to find him through the Internet."

"There are such men and women everywhere, Jacqueline," Reiniger said. "They are enamored with the mysteries of magic and alchemy, mysteries that speak to them in a way modern science does not. As they should be, of course."

"As they say today, he is your number-one fan," the woman—Jacqueline—said.

Reiniger laughed. "Indeed. Once I convinced him I truly am Paracelsus, whom he has long idolized, it was easy to sway him to my side by offering him the secret of the Philosopher's Stone, the source of eternal youth and endless wealth."

"As that secret swayed me to your side, when you found me in the Emperor Napoleon's court," said Jacqueline. "Though it was not the only thing that swayed me to your side."

Whoa, I thought. *Talk about someone spry for her age. And also, yuck.*

And then I thought, *So, Dr. Ballard sold his Grade 7 science class to Paracelsus for money and eternal youth.* There was only one word for someone like that., and it was another word Dad would have grounded me for if he'd heard me say it out loud.

Paracelsus and his Parisian paramour—a word I'd only learned a few weeks before and was proud of having found such an alliterative use for—paused outside my room. I couldn't tell if they could see me or not, so I stayed still. "Nor will Dr. Ballard's usefulness end when I am done my work here," Reiniger continued. "He will be blamed for everything, while I will quietly resign and slip away to grieve my just-deceased wife."

I felt a surge of savage approval. *They're going to frame Dr. Ballard for what happened—make him the fall guy,* I thought, even though that turn of phrase was more appropriate to an old gangster flick than the horror movie I was currently living in. I wasn't sure *how* they intended to do that, but it wouldn't hurt my feelings to see my science teacher go to jail.

Assuming I lived that long.

"*Oui,* very neat," said the woman.

The door opened. There was a pause. *They must be looking at me,* I thought.

"Should not she be waking up?" the woman said.

"She should," said Reiniger. "It is time."

I felt a chill. *Time for what?*

Footsteps came to the side of the bed. A hand grabbed my chin and turned my face toward the ceiling. I kept my eyes closed, but something popped, and a sharp, pungent odour entered my nose and my brain. I gasped, then coughed. After that, there was no point pretending I was anything other than awake, so I opened my eyes and glared at Vice-Principal Reiniger in his ridiculous mask. "I know who you are," I said. "You can take off the mask."

He shrugged. "As you wish." He pulled it off and set it aside, revealing the square-jawed, blue-eyed face I remembered from school, one icy glare from which was all it took to stop anyone from running in the hall. "It has been useful for terrorizing your classmates and keeping them quiescent, but you are quite right, I do not need it with you."

He sat beside me on the edge of the bed and put his right hand on my forehead. I tried to jerk away from his touch but had nowhere to go. He simply pressed harder, pinning my head in place. He closed his eyes for a moment. "Yes," he said. "Yes. I was not mistaken. It is strong in her. She is a natural." He opened his eyes again. "That fool, Ballard . . . I told him I wanted her most of all. He should have delayed the bus trip until she was well enough to accompany the class."

"A natural what?" I said. "And keep your hands to yourself!"

But he not only kept his right hand on my forehead, he gripped my shoulder with his left hand, and then . . .

In my whole life, the sickest I'd ever felt was the night I spent very close to my new best friend, the toilet, after eating the bad burrito that had fortuitously kept me from the Grade 7 science field trip.

Until now.

"It felt like he was pulling my insides out through my ears," Lorenzo had said.

Maybe to him. To me, it felt like he was pulling my stomach and heart and lungs and kidneys and liver and intestines and all those other gross slimy interior things up and out through my throat. *Wrong* and *disgusting*, Lorenzo's other words for the experience, didn't begin to touch it. My mouth gaped wide and I choked and I knew I was about to throw up all over myself—

—and then I wasn't even *in* myself.

I felt a moment of profound relief as the awful sick-making sensation vanished as if someone had thrown a switch, then a moment of profound disorientation, because all of a sudden, I was standing in the far corner of the room, next to the overturned office chair, staring at Reiniger, who was leaning over a motionless body on a cot.

Wait a second, I thought. *I recognize that body. That's my body!*

Then I thought, *Am I really that skinny?*

And then I thought, *But if I'm over there, how can I be . . .?*

I looked down. I still had a body, and it was very bit as skinny as the body in the bed—but rather than flesh and bone and skin, it was made of clear water.

I lifted my hand and looked right through it at Reiniger's distorted image. I made a fist of water, then opened it again.

The movement attracted Jacqueline's gaze. Her eyes widened, and she gasped. "Paracelsus! Look!" She pointed.

Reiniger turned his gaze in my direction. His own eyes widened. I took a step toward him, wanting to pull his hateful hands from the body in the bed. He jerked away from it . . .

. . . and suddenly I was back *in* that body, my real body, my flesh-and-blood body, while water splashed to the floor where I had been standing just a moment before. The nausea returned full-force and I just had time to turn my head before I really did throw up, over the side of the bed, which was every bit as awful as it sounds, although I got some enjoyment out of the fact that Reiniger did not scramble up fast enough to entirely avoid being splattered.

The bad taste in my mouth when I'd woken up was nothing compared to the bad taste in my mouth now. Swallowing and wishing desperately for water—ironically enough, considering what I had momentarily become—I turned my head back and closed my eyes, breathing hard and thinking harder. *He turned me into an elemental. A water-*

elemental—a nymph. But Lorenzo said it took many tries to turn him into a fire-elemental!

I opened my eyes again to see Reiniger staring down at me. "Astonishing," he breathed. He glanced at Jacqueline. "Absolutely astonishing!"

She, too, was staring at me. "Have you *ever* turned a subject that quickly before?"

"Only once, half a century before we met. It was a great moment for me. The boy became a salamander, like Lorenzo is becoming, and for many years he was my most loyal and powerful servant, until his energies dissipated." He looked down at me again, his face eager. "This one could be just as powerful! She formed a water body without a source of water at hand, drawing it out of the air. Amazing!"

I glared at him. "Powerful, maybe, but never *loyal*," I snarled.

He chuckled. "You won't have a choice, little girl. The elementals I create, I control."

Not Lorenzo, I thought, remembering how Lorenzo had managed to temporarily escape, how he had fought and defeated Paracelsus's other nymphs and an earth-elemental at my house.

Then I felt a chill. Paracelsus had to know what Lorenzo had done. What had he done to Lorenzo in turn? *Where is Lorenzo now?*

"A salamander," I said. "That's a fire-elemental."

His eyelids lifted. "Correct, but how do *you* know that?"

"There's this thing called Google. All the kids are using it these days. Try to keep up."

He snorted. "Childish defiance and insult will avail you nothing. I have created hundreds of elementals in my long, long life. Many children have been as 'brave' as you. Others have wept or prayed. A few, taken from the lower classes, have screamed obscenities and curses and sworn to wreak vengeance on me once they were elementals. It is all, as Solomon puts it in *Ecclesiastes*, 'vanity and a striving after wind.' All, once they were fully formed, served me, unable to resist my will. Very few even tried, and those that did soon ceased, because after a few short weeks in elemental form, their human will, mind, and individuality vanished completely—as will yours."

"So how about Lorenzo?" I said. "He's not exactly been doing what you tell him, has he? He even turned himself into an elemental." No point in pretending I didn't know what had happened at my own house. "Maybe you're losing your touch."

"I have stopped him from being able to make himself into a salamander," Paracelsus said. "I admit, he surprised me, developing that ability, but it is not the first time I have encountered it. I have given him a drug that prevents him from doing it again. His defiance will cease once he is permanently a salamander. And that day will come soon." He smiled; it wasn't a pleasant smile, even though his teeth were even and white. Was it my imagination, or did he look younger than I remembered him? "As will the day when you become a nymph forever. You converted into one so easily, I may be able to make that happen almost immediately."

The smile slipped away. He leaned forward and said, in a low, poisonous voice, "Your friend Meg raged at me too, swore at me, cursed me in language that in my youth would have shocked the hardest sailor. But now she lies immobilized and gagged. She, too, has the elemental force within her. It has taken three attempts, and like you, she was violently ill . . ."(I gritted my teeth, hearing that) ". . . but on my last try, she made a very creditable sylph. Soon she, too, will be mine. Two others of your classmates will make creditable earth-elementals, if I have time to develop them: they are border-line, at best. The rest . . ." He shrugged. "Those, I will soon finish draining of life-force. It will be enough to keep me and my lovely wife young for another four or five decades."

"That will kill them!"

"Of course it will, and there is absolutely nothing *you* can do to stop it. Think on that, *all* of that, and abandon your defiance, foolish girl. Your time would be better spent praying that God will still accept your tainted soul when it at last it slips away from your elemental body." He turned away. "Come, Jacqueline."

His wife gave me a poisonous smile and then followed him out into the common room.

I tugged at the straps again, harder than ever, but it was useless. He's going to kill them! All my friends . . .

Melanie. Pyotr, the littlest boy in the class, who had shaggy black hair and bright-blue eyes and a thick Russian accent all the girls—including me—found adorable. Quiet Lisa, who barely spoke in class but had the highest grades of all of us. Stephen, whose smile lit up his dark-skinned face whenever he was happy, which was most of the time. Nick, who'd teased me on the playground when we were little and thought he knew everything about everything when really, he knew very little about anything except hockey. All the others...

Even Nick *doesn't deserve to end up as a desiccated mummy at the hands of the vice-principal,* I thought, and felt sick, and furious, and maybe most of all, embarrassed—embarrassed at having been caught so easily, like a stupid little kid. *That's all you are,* I told myself viciously. *Just a dumb, useless kid. A little girl, playing 'let's pretend,' imagining you could take on an ancient alchemist.*

Then I told myself to shut up, because I don't let *anybody* talk to me like that, and it wasn't helping. I went back to trying to figure out how to break free of my straps . . . with no more success than the first twelve times I'd tugged at them.

Finally, sore and tired, I quit trying. I stared at the stained acoustic tile on the former office's ceiling, and the unlit fluorescent light, one tube missing, dangling above my head.

I thought back to those few moments I'd been a nymph. I hadn't *felt* as if Reiniger had had control of me: I'd felt free. Confused and a little dazed, yes—but I'd actually taken a step toward him before he'd broken the connection with my real body and I'd been sucked back into it.

Lorenzo learned to move around without permission. Why can't I? Especially since I'm apparently a 'natural?' The next time I'm a nymph, I can rush Paracelsus, knock him down, knock him out, then . . .

Then what? that nasty, nattering, naysaying part of me asked mockingly. *The minute you knock him down you'll end up back in your body, still tied to the bed.*

Maybe I can free myself before that happens.

Big maybe.

I told myself again to shut up because I was getting annoying, and closed my eyes, mustering my strength. When Paracelsus came back, I'd be ready.

Except my little elemental excursion had totally exhausted me. Which meant the next time someone came into the room, far from being ready, I was sound asleep.

The first I knew about my visitor was a voice. "Oh, no," it said. "Sam. What are you doing here?"

I opened eyes so gummy I had to blink them half a dozen

times to clearly see the face of the speaker, but I already knew who he was. I'd heard that voice a hundred times, as it taught me the finer points of photosynthesis and electricity and digestion.

"Hello, Dr. Ballard," I said, trying to make every word drip venom. "Nice of you to drop by."

CHAPTER 21
I DO SOMETHING UNEXPECTED

"Oh, Sam," Dr. Ballard said sadly, "I never wanted *you* to end up like this."

"Unlike Lorenzo? Unlike Pyotr and Melanie and all the others?" I have been angry once or twice in my life (Dad says I have his mother's temper, but since I never knew her, I can't judge—Grandma in Victoria is Mom's mom, and I've never heard a single harsh word from her), but my fury in that moment outdid every burst of temper I'd ever experienced before. Even though my elemental form was apparently water, I felt like I could have burst into flame like Lorenzo with just a touch more effort.

Dr. Ballard looked down. "Sacrifices are necessary for the advancement of science."

"Science?" I glared at him, but apparently, death rays out of my eyes weren't part of the nymph package either. "There's no science going on here. It's all magic."

Dr. Ballard's head snapped up again. I'd apparently hit a nerve. "There's no such thing!" In his voice, I heard the same fervour he'd had telling me about Paracelsus in the lab after we'd followed him into the school. "There are only natural laws we don't yet understand. Don't you see, Sam? Paracelsus has lived for *centuries*. He knows how to create *elementals*. If I can figure out the science behind his abilities and harness it, think of what it could mean to the world!"

"He's lived for centuries by sucking the life out of *children*!" I cried. "He makes elementals out of *children*!"

"Only because he does it in a non-scientific manner," Dr. Ballard said as though he were explaining something self-evident to a particularly stupid student—which I'd never been, so I resented it. "It's like . . . look, the ancients knew that an extract from willow bark could relieve pain. But it wasn't until science came along that the pain-relieving chemical in willow bark, salicylic acid, was identified and isolated, and it wasn't until 1853 that a chemist produced acetylsalicylic acid, which became known as Aspirin, the drug that made that pain relief available to everyone. And it wasn't until 1971, more than a century later, that scientists figured out *how* it worked."

I stared at him. I was a prisoner, strapped to a cot, facing a complete and irreversible conversion into a nymph—and he was giving me a science lesson.

Maybe my disbelief showed on my face because he hurried on. "The point is, if I can learn what's really going on when he 'drains the life force' out of someone or creates an elemental out of them, then maybe I can make those abilities available to *everyone*. We could learn to extend life without having to steal it from children, or how to create elementals as powerful tools to . . . to build dams, or for search and rescue, or to extinguish fires. I hate the fact you kids are suffering, and I've done my best to make everyone as comfortable as possible—but think what this suffering could ultimately lead to: nothing less than a world where no one would ever die of old age!"

None of us *will die of old age*, I thought. If I hadn't been strapped down, I'd have kicked him somewhere sensitive. I wondered if he really believed what he was telling me or if he was just justifying his actions to himself.

"Maybe," I said. "But *you* won't be around to see it."

He blinked at me. "What?"

"I overheard Vice-Principal Reiniger and his definitely-*not*-dying wife talking about you. *You* don't get to live forever. You don't even get to follow Reiniger around and study him if that's what you really want to do. They've arranged things so that you're going to take the blame for the disappearance of your entire Grade 7 science class." And I suddenly realized what that really meant. I'd thought they were just going to get him arrested . . . but they couldn't have him trying to tell the cops he hadn't really done anything, and they should be investigating Vice-Principal Reiniger instead, could they? "They're going to kill you!" I blurted. I'd been fine with him going to jail, but I didn't want him *dead*.

Dr. Ballard's mouth fell open, not something I'd seen happen very often in real life, even though it seems to happen to characters in books all the time. He stared at me for a second, then said, "You're lying."

"Why would I lie?"

"To get me to help you."

"Will you?"

"No."

"So why would I lie?"

I had him there. He stared at me a moment longer, then turned and left the room without unstrapping me and telling me to run out of the compound and go find the police, which was, to be honest, kind of what I was hoping for.

Great, I thought. *There goes that chance.*

Since I was still strapped to the bed and clearly not going anywhere, I went back to thinking about those moments when I was a nymph. Somehow, I and some of the other kids —including Lorenzo and Meg—had something inside us that could form an elemental. Unlike Dr. Ballard, I didn't care about the scientific explanation, if there really was one. All that mattered was that somehow Reiniger—Paracelsus—had learned how to pull the inner elementals out of the kids that had them.

No, that wasn't quite right. What *mattered* was that Lorenzo had figured out how to turn himself into an elemental without Paracelsus's "help." Which meant Paracelsus wasn't in as complete control as he thought he was.

I frowned. But for some reason, Lorenzo couldn't go just anywhere—he could only come to where I was. Because he and I, for some reason, had a connection . . .

Never mind why, I thought hastily. *The point is Lorenzo can operate as an elemental out of Paracelsus's control. And anything he can do, I can do.*

In fact, I already had. I'd taken a step toward Paracelsus before he even realized I'd become a nymph. Maybe he *could* control elementals just through the force of his will, but based on what I'd seen, he had to be very focused to do so—and I'd taken him by surprise.

If I could turn *myself* into a nymph *and* take him by surprise . . .

Jacqueline suddenly appeared in the doorway. "Making my rounds, *ma chère,*" she said. "Do you need to go to the bathroom? Speak now, or wet the bed later because I will not be checking on you again tonight."

Tonight . . .

"What time is it?" I said.

"Almost an hour after midnight."

"Yes," I said. "I need to go."

"Do not try anything foolish," she warned me as she came over to the bed, avoiding the smelly puddle of vomit but making no move to clean it up. She held up something I didn't recognize but which somehow looked mean.

"What is that?"

"Taser," she said. "This modern age, it has so *many* wonderful inventions. When I first began helping Paracelsus with the harvesting of elementals and, more importantly, the keeping of both of us young, I had to hit children with clubs. This is *so* much more civilized."

Holding the Taser in her right hand, she used her left to awkwardly undo the straps. I swung my legs over the side and stood up, the concrete floor cold under my bare feet, glad to stretch my legs.

I looked around: not a bathroom in sight, which wasn't too surprising in what had originally been an office. "Where do I go?"

"This way." She grabbed my left arm and propelled me out the door.

The office did not open directly into the big common room. Instead, I found myself in a hallway, lit only by a red EXIT sign still burning at one end and a dim fluorescent glow through a propped-open door near that sign. The rest of the doors along the corridor were closed.

Jacqueline dragged me down the hallway to the open door. "In there," she said and pushed me through.

Urinals hung on the walls. "This is the men's room."

"I assure you no men will be coming in to pee. Get on with it. I am tired."

I went into one of the two stalls and tried to hold my breath while I did what I was there for. Like the toilet in the bathroom I had hidden in earlier, this one did not appear to have been cleaned for the past several decades.

Rust-coloured water spouted from the tap in the sink when I went to wash my hands. Ice-cold, of course. Also, there was no soap and no paper towels. I rinsed my hands as best I could, then wiped them on the thin fabric of my hospital gown.

Jacqueline grabbed my arm the minute I came out the door and almost dragged me back down the hallway. She pushed me flat on the bed and strapped me down again. She had to holster the Taser while she did it, but she was bigger than me and much stronger than I would have expected— maybe not surprising since she, like Reiniger, had clearly extended her life by sucking the youth out of children. There was no way I could overpower her and run away, though the thought did cross my mind (TV and movies, again).

"*Bon nuit,*" she said. "Sleep tight. I would say, 'Do not let the bedbugs bite,' but in this place, from what the other children have told me, there is little you can do about *that.*"

She went to the door and turned out the light, plunging the room into darkness, just barely alleviated by what little of the light from the EXIT sign and open men's room made it down that far and through the window.

I will not cry, I told myself fiercely as she went out and closed the door behind her, and her footsteps click-clacked down the hall. *I will not cry*.

I cried.

But only for a little while. Because then, I focused my mind on something other than my miserable condition: trying to remember *exactly* what I had felt when Paracelsus had turned me into a nymph. At the time, I'd felt so sick I hadn't been able to notice anything else, but thinking back, I was able to tease out what else I had felt: a weird sensation in my head, as though Paracelsus had turned a valve in my brain and all of the stuff that made me, well, *me* had stopped flowing along its usual . . . pipes, for want of a better word, and instead, had suddenly flowed somewhere else: right out of my body, and into the water-body that had sprung into existence in the corner of the room.

I thought hard about that strange sensation, harder than I'd thought about anything ever, concentrating so fiercely I no longer felt the straps chafing my wrists and ankles or the air chilling my thinly clad body. It was almost like dreaming, but I wasn't asleep: I was chasing something inside my own brain, something that seemed to be trying to hide from me, but finally, I thought I could feel it, see it, almost, a girl-shape —*my* shape—and I mentally seized it, and pulled it to me, and . . .

. . . and just like that, I was standing in the corner of the office again, in the dark, in a shape made of water, staring at the barely visible, immobile lump that was my real body on the bed.

CHAPTER 22
I GO FOR A WALK

I looked down at myself. Yep, made of water. I took a tentative step to see if I truly was in control of this new body. I was.

I didn't feel heat or cold, just weight and pressure. I knew there was solid stone beneath my feet, but that was all. I took another step, and then another, and then I was standing by the bed, looking down at my "real" body. Its—my—eyes were closed, and I could see my chest rising and falling . . .

Which was also when I realized I could see in the dark. *Well, why not? It's not like I really have eyes, do I?*

I looked around. Everything was in shades of black and white, like footage from an old security camera. I glanced back at my sleeping body. I could feel a kind of . . . tug from it. Nymph-me wanted back inside human-me, and I had a feeling that desire would just keep growing until I couldn't stand it anymore. Which meant I couldn't stay a nymph indefinitely . . .

. . . at least, not until Paracelsus made me one forever. I had an inkling of what that would feel like now. Cut off from my flesh-and-blood body, but always longing to rejoin it . . . it must drive the permanent elementals insane! As it would me and Lorenzo and Meg and all the others if Reiniger succeeded.

But right now, that tug back to my body was just a slight annoyance, like a pebble in a shoe. I could stand it a little longer.

I reached out with watery fingers. Were they solid enough to . . .?

They were. With the same dexterity I would have had with my real fingers, I unbuckled the straps holding my arms and legs but left them loosely in place so it wouldn't be immediately apparent to someone coming in that I wasn't secured.

Then I stepped out through the door into the hallway.

I was still getting used to the feeling of being a nymph. I'd identified the tug my real body exerted on my nymph body. But now, as I rummaged around inside my watery head, I felt something else . . . another kind of tug, much fainter than the one trying to pull me back into my own flesh and bone, like a string I could follow to . . . somewhere.

And I thought I knew where.

Lorenzo.

The thread that connected him to me also connected me to him. *Does that mean . . .?*

No time to worry about that right now. Instead, I concentrated on that barely-there sensation.

Suddenly, I saw something, a glowing thread imposing itself on my vision, a line of light leading straight down the hall toward the EXIT sign, and I *knew* that at the other end of it, I'd find Lorenzo.

I started down the hallway. The door marked EXIT

opened easily and, as I'd suspected, led into the main common room. The fiery thread in my mind pointed me to another door on the far side of the room. Again, I could see the entire space in shades of grey, including the kitchen behind its long counter, the bags of chips and loaves of bread, the stacked plates, and the scattered tables and overturned chairs.

The door to which the glowing string in my mind led me opened into another corridor, longer than the one in which my old-office cell was located, with three doors opening off to either side. Bulletin boards on the walls sported a handful of childish drawings. Glancing through an open door, I saw tiny tables with tiny benches and realized this must have been the daycare/school for the survivalist compound. I wondered where those kids were now . . . and realized with a shock they'd be my grandma's age.

At least they got to grow up and get old, I thought. *Unlike us, if I don't stop Paracelsus.*

A little way farther, the corridor was interrupted by two swinging doors. A sign above the door read DORMITORY. I pushed my watery way through the right-hand door and found myself in yet another corridor, running to my right and left. There were two more signs, one pointing right that read GIRLS, and one pointing left that read BOYS. There was no sound from either direction to indicate the presence of any of my classmates, but the fiery thread went right into the GIRLS side. There were about a dozen doors down that way; the thread disappeared under the first door on the left.

Unlike the door that had taken me into the old rec room Melanie was in, this one had a simple sliding bolt holding it locked from this side. I slid it aside, opened the door, stepped through . . .

. . . and there was Lorenzo.

I would have gasped if I'd had lungs. He lay on his side on a cot just like the one I'd been on, but he wasn't strapped down, and he had a blanket, which was more than they'd given me. He stirred as I came in and sat up suddenly, eyes wide and white in my strange black-and-white vision, the blanket slipping off the side of the cot to puddle on the floor as he did so. All he was wearing was pyjama bottoms, and he looked way skinnier than the last time I'd seen him in the flesh, his ribs almost as visible as the ribs of the skeleton in Dr. Ballard's laboratory. The glowing thread in my mind ended where he sat.

I took a step toward him, and he pushed back so fast that his bare back made a slapping sound against the wall. I suddenly realized he couldn't recognize me: I was a nymph, and his last few encounters with those hadn't exactly been friendly.

I stopped in frustration. Could I talk? I wasn't sure. "Lorenzo," I tried saying. "It's me, Sam."

Even in my own . . . ears, I guess . . . my voice sounded strange, gurgling and bubbling like a broken water fountain. But I'd definitely formed words.

"Sam?" Lorenzo's eyes widened, and then, to my horror, tears welled up in them, sparkling in my nymph vision. "Oh, no, Sam, no. He got you, too?"

I nodded, realized he might not be able to see it, and added, "Yes."

"How long . . .?"

"He caught me a few hours ago."

"A few . . .?" Lorenzo blinked. "But that's . . . you're already . . . it took him days to make me . . ."

"He says I'm a natural," I said uncomfortably. "He was

upset I wasn't on the trip. He'd wanted me most of all, apparently."

"Then . . . the attack was planned all along?"

"Yes."

"So Dr. Ballard *is* Paracelsus?"

"No," I said. "I was wrong. He's just a . . . minion." *There* was a word I'd never before used outside discussions centred around certain animated films. "Paracelsus is Mr. Reiniger."

"The vice-principal?"

"Yes."

"But . . . why? What is he trying to do?"

I opened my mouth to explain, but all the time we'd been talking, the tug back to my body had been growing—and all at once, in a rush, it couldn't be denied anymore. Just like that, Lorenzo's room vanished.

I gasped, my arms and legs stiffened, my eyes flew open, and I found myself back in my real body: my cold, sore, stiff, flesh-and-blood body.

I stared up at the dark light fixture over my head, barely visible to my human eyes in the dim light. Had it all been a dream?

My nose itched. Without thinking, I lifted a hand to scratch it—and my hand pulled free of the unbuckled strap.

No, it hadn't been a dream.

And that meant I didn't have to wait to turn into a nymph again to move around the compound.

I finished scratching my nose—first things first—then jerked free of the other straps, sat up, swung my bare feet down onto the cold concrete, avoiding the vomit puddle, and padded to the hallway. I looked both ways along it—still deserted.

I trotted down to the door under the EXIT sign and eased

it open. The space beyond was far darker than it had been when I was in nymph form, the four lights that had been on earlier apparently having been switched off by Jacqueline, but I could see well enough to pick my way across the open space through the overturned chairs. Nameless grit dug painfully into the bottoms of my feet, and I hoped I wouldn't suddenly find some broken glass or rusty nails.

Soles still intact, I pushed through the door into the school corridor, walked down it, pushed through the swinging doors into the dormitory hall, went into the room where I'd found Lorenzo . . .

. . . and there he was, just as I'd seen him minutes before, except he'd picked up that blanket and draped it over his bare shoulders. "Sam?" he breathed. "For real this time?"

I ran over to him and finally gave him the hug I would have given him the first time I saw him in salamander form if not for the third-degree burn risk. He hugged me back, hard. His body felt painfully thin in my arms. "We have to get out of here," I said, pulling away.

"I don't know if I can walk," he said. "I feel weak and kind of dizzy. There's . . . a shot they've been giving me. I don't know what it is . . ."

"A drug to keep you from turning yourself into a fire elemental," I said grimly. "Reiniger told me."

Lorenzo gave me an odd look. "You seem to have had a long talk with him."

"It was mostly one-sided. Look, you can lean on me. If we can get out, we'll go to the police. You were on the bus. They'll believe *you*."

"Okay, I'll try," Lorenzo said. He swung his legs over the bed. I put my arm around his blanket-draped shoulders and tried to help him stand . . .

. . . but his eyes rolled back in his head, and he dropped back down again. If I hadn't caught him, he would have slid right off the bed.

His head flopped forward, then he jerked it up again and swallowed hard. He looked at me and shook his head. "It's no good. Not yet. They gave me the last shot just an hour ago. Maybe if we can wait . . ."

"But we *can't* wait. We'll get caught!"

"Then you have to go without me."

"The police won't believe me," I said desperately. "I've already tried."

"Your house was wrecked by *something*. And if you're here now, you must have been missing ever since."

"They *are* searching for me," I said. "I saw them."

"There you are," Loreno said. "This time, they'll listen. They have to."

"Well, maybe," I said. If Lorenzo was too weak to escape, what choice did I have? "Will you be all right?"

"Just hurry," Lorenzo said. He sounded scared. I hated it. "Paracelsus says next time he changes me, he'll make it permanent."

"So attack him as soon as you're an elemental," I said. "Before he can finish whatever he's doing. He can't control you. You've proved that already."

"Yes, he *can*," Lorenzo said. "When he really focuses his will on you, it's impossible to resist. I only escaped because he didn't know about my connection to you. But if he turns all his attention on me, he can command me to do . . . anything. Maybe even hurt you or someone else."

"He can't control *me*," I said fiercely.

"He hasn't really tried," Lorenzo said. "You haven't felt it.

Sam. Please. Don't underestimate him. Get out. Get help. *Real help.*"

I swallowed. "Okay." I gave him another awkward hug. "Be safe," I said.

"A little late for that," Lorenzo whispered into my ear. His breath tickled. "But I'll try."

I let him go, blinking back tears. "'Bye," I said.

Then I ran for the door, heading back to the common room.

There, I hesitated. The EXIT sign glowed above the stairs, pointing the way to freedom. But it felt wrong to just go off and leave everyone else strapped to their beds, waiting for who knew what.

Some will be like Lorenzo. Too weak to run. They'll slow me down too much. I can't take them with me. Except . . .

My heart leaped. *Meg! Meg won't be too weak. She's only been here a little longer than me!*

But even as I thought it, I realized I couldn't rescue her, either. The trouble was, she could be anywhere. She might be in one of the old dorm rooms, she might not. Melanie hadn't been, and I'd been put in an old office. Everyone was probably scattered all over the bunker. I couldn't search every room, and the longer I tried, the more likely I'd make a sound, or someone else would, bringing Jacqueline and her Taser running.

I'm so sorry, Meg! I cried inwardly. Then I hurried across the common room to the stairs. I climbed them, ran through the shorter hallways at the top, reached the main staircase to the outside, and clambered up them as fast as I could. I was panting by the time I reached the door to the outside.

It was closed. I'd left it open. Someone had used it.

The door had a push bar on this side. I pushed with all my

strength, grunting as the heavy door swung up and over and crashed down, and then I was out.

I took a deep breath of the cold night air, trying to rid my lungs of the omnipresent musty, stale stench of the bunker down below. When I exhaled, I could see my breath in the starlight. My skin had already erupted in goosebumps beneath the thin cloth of the hospital gown, and icy dew had drenched my feet. I had to keep moving, not only to escape but to keep from freezing to death. I had to get back to the highway, flag down a car, get into town, get to the police, make them believe me.

They'd *have* to believe me. As Lorenzo had said, *something* had wrecked my house, and *I* clearly hadn't done it. I'd been a missing person ever since. If I turned up now, no matter how crazy my story sounded, they'd at least check it out— and this time, I could lead them straight to the back door. The kids would still be in the complex—there was no way they could evacuated and taken anywhere else in so short a time. Heck, with luck, the odious Jacqueline wouldn't even know I was missing until she made her morning rounds. Dr. Ballard and Reiniger/Paracelsus had probably gone back into town— that was probably why the back door was closed.

I started across the compound to the place where the fence had been partially knocked down by the St. Bernard-sized boulder. Maybe I could climb over the fence there, then circle around to the . . .

Someone grabbed me from behind.

CHAPTER 23
I CUT SHORT A SLEEPOVER

I screamed and struggled, but whoever held me was too big and too strong for me to break away. "How'd you get out?" a voice said roughly, and I recognized Dr. Ballard.

I went limp, panting. "I'm smarter than you," I said. (Weaker snark than I usually manage, but I wasn't at my best.)

"And where did you think you'd go?" Dr. Ballard went on. "It would take you hours to get back to town. You'd freeze to death."

"I just have to get to the road."

"No traffic this time of night. You'd still freeze to death."

"Let me go, and we'll find out, won't we?"

Dr. Ballard sighed. "Sam, I really wish I could. I was glad when you got food poisoning that day—"

"Gee, thanks."

"—because you were my favourite student, with such great potential. I hated the thought of seeing it snuffed out."

"Just not enough to, you know, not go ahead with the whole getting-your-class-kidnapped thing."

"I already explained that. The potential knowledge to be gained by—"

"Tell it to the cops."

His grip tightened. "Fine," he said. "Be that way. Let's go back down. Paracelsus will want to know how you escaped."

"I thought he'd left." I squirmed uselessly. "I thought *you'd* left."

"I'm camped out here." Dr. Ballard turned me around—literally picked me up and set me down again—and I saw for the first time the pale lump of a tent on the rise leading up to the shelf of rock above the collapsed garage entrance. "Keeping watch. Good thing, huh?"

He forced me back across the compound to the door. I fought him again there, trying to squirm free. I'd twist out of the hospital gown, leave him holding it, and run away in my underwear if I had to. I had to be faster than him; he was old . . .

. . . but he was also strong, and his arm across my chest tightened so much I could barely breathe, and my squirming just . . . stopped.

Then I thought of my nymph form, but I couldn't find my way into it, not with my physical body being manhandled—literally. In the end, I had no choice but to make my reluctant way back down the stairs into the complex I'd been so close to escaping, my hopes of rescue dwindling with every step.

Once we were down in the darkened common room, he led me through yet another door into yet another corridor—this one, for a wonder, well-lit. The doors here were much farther apart, and the floor was carpeted in pale blue rather than being tile or bare concrete. Artwork even hung on the walls (ugly artwork—one was obviously a paint-by-number landscape).

Dr. Ballard stopped at the second door on the right and knocked on it sharply. Nobody answered.

"Guess they've left," I said. "Maybe we should come back later."

"Shut up, Sam." He knocked again.

The door opened. Jacqueline stood there, wearing a white robe, her feet tucked into fuzzy pink slippers. "What?" she said. Then her eyes fell on me and widened. She reached out and snapped on a light in the entryway beyond the door, so sudden and bright it made me wince. "How did she get free?"

"My question exactly," Dr. Ballard said dryly.

"And mine," said Paracelsus. Like Jacqueline, he wore a robe, his legs bare beneath it, his feet in more masculine slippers of dark red velvet. Since I was in a hospital gown, Dr. Ballard was the only one fully dressed.

It's like a pyjama party in hell, I thought.

Paracelsus glared at me. "Well?"

"I kept pulling at the straps, and eventually, one of them came loose," I said. "And the door wasn't locked. Jacqueline should be more careful."

Jacqueline slapped me. No warning; her hand just lashed out across my face so hard my head jerked around to the right, and my ears rang. "You will be respectful," she snarled.

"Dear Jacqueline does not believe you," Paracelsus said. "Nor do I. Those straps would not give way. Someone had to unfasten them . . ." Then his eyes widened. "Lorenzo! I thought I had stopped him from . . . we must go check. Bring her!"

He brushed past me and Dr. Ballard. Dr. Ballard pushed me after him. Jacqueline followed, cinching her robe tighter. "Are you saying Lorenzo freed her?" Dr. Ballard said to

Paracelsus's back. "I thought you controlled these elementals."

"I do," said Paracelsus without looking around. We stepped out into the common room and headed across it. "But sometimes, an elemental, while his purity is still polluted by his physical body, feels an emotional connection to some friend or family member—enough of a connection that the elemental can act independently. It can travel along that connection to wherever that other person is. I have dealt with such complications before. I did not expect Lorenzo to have such a connection—it is rare to find it among children, especially in this modern age—but he does to this girl. He has been able to convert into salamander form on his own and visit her a handful of times. I thought the drug I have been giving him would prevent him from doing so again. Perhaps her being so much closer allowed it." He twisted his head around to look at me. "That's what happened, isn't it? Lorenzo freed you."

No, sucker, I thought, but out loud, all I said was, "What will you do to him?"

"It is time he became my servant in all things," Paracelsus said, facing front again. We reached the door into the school corridor. "I intended to wait until tomorrow, but under the circumstances, I am willing to—what is the expression you brats use?—oh, yes, 'pull an all-nighter.' It is time to put an end to all this." He pushed through the swinging doors into the dormitory hallway.

My heart jumped in my chest. "Put an end to it *how*?"

"What do you think?" he said with withering contempt. Just outside the closed door into the room where I'd left Lorenzo, he turned to face me. "The elementals that can be made permanent will be. Lorenzo, you, and Meg, for certain;

Nick and Pyotr . . . more doubtful, but perhaps. The others, I will drain of their remaining life force. Then, I will have the earth elementals finish the destruction of this place. No one will ever find any of the bodies. The whereabouts of the missing children will remain a mystery for all time."

"*Bodies?*" Dr. Ballard grabbed my shoulders and pulled me back toward him protectively.

Paracelsus gave him an irritated look. "What is it now?"

"You told me you would take some life force from the children, but you would leave them alive," he said. "You said you would arrange to have them found once we had moved on to continue our research elsewhere. In time, you said, they would recover."

I twisted my head around, trying to see Dr. Ballard's face, thinking, *How naïve can you be?*

"And this is why you have been doting on them," Jacqueline said in her heavy French accent. "It has been most amusing to see you feeding them and washing their clothes and even giving them books and games. Such a waste of time, it has all been. You could have left them in squalor and filth, and it would have made no difference in the end."

I do not like that woman, I thought.

"You always knew that those who became elementals would leave their bodies behind," Paracelsus said. "Their dead bodies. You accepted that from the beginning."

Dr. Ballard's hands tightened on my shoulders. It hurt. "Yes. I understand the necessity. But the others . . . you promised." Dr. Ballard sounded like a little kid who had been refused ice cream.

"Circumstances have changed," Paracelsus said. "It is no longer possible to leave any of children capable of telling tales we do not want to be told." He took a step, soft but somehow threatening, toward Dr. Ballard. "Do we have a problem?"

Jacqueline moved into view from behind us. Her Taser had appeared in her hand.

Dr. Ballard's hands tightened even more, making me wince—but then, all at once, they relaxed. He released me and stepped back. "No," he said quietly. "Forgive me. I am suffering from vestigial sentimentality, unbecoming of a scientist. Nothing more. Of course, the work is too important to leave any loose ends that might interfere with it. It must continue."

Paracelsus regarded him narrowly, then nodded once. "We'll say no more about it." He glanced at me. "I will begin with Lorenzo. Put the girl in with her friend. They can talk about boys. Braid each other's hair, perhaps . . . while they still have it." He chuckled nastily, then pointed to one of the closed doors down the hall to the right. "There."

Dr. Ballard took my arm and pulled me down the hall to the indicated door while Paracelsus and Jacqueline went into Lorenzo's room. Holding me tight against him with his left arm, Dr. Ballard unbolted and opened the door with his right. Then he pushed me through so hard I stumbled and fell, banging my knees painfully on the tile floor. As I struggled back to my feet, he turned on the light.

The room was larger than the one Lorenzo was in. Rather than a dorm room, it looked like it had been the girls' common room, with a kitchen counter in the corner, complete with toaster-oven, an old refrigerator, and a round table with four chairs at it. A ratty-looking couch and a couple of matching armchairs had been pushed up against the wall, out of the way of two cots identical to the one I'd been strapped to in the old office where I'd unwillingly discovered my inner nymph.

Meg lay on the one nearest the door. Like me, she wore a hospital gown. Unlike me, she was still strapped down. A spot of blood showed on a bandage wrapped around her head, a cut from the car accident, I guessed. Dr. Ballard must have bandaged it—it seemed clear neither Paracelsus or Jacqueline would have bothered, just as they had not bothered to do anything about the barbed-wire scratch on my leg, which was covered in dried blood as well as caked with dirt. I hoped it didn't get infected. I hoped I lived long enough to worry about it.

Meg's eyes opened, blinked—and then, finally, focused on me. "Sam?"

"Meg," I said. "Long time no see."

Her eyes flicked to Dr. Ballard. "He's not Paracelsus."

"Yeah," I said. "I know." I tried to grin. "Told you so."

Dr. Ballard dragged me to the second cot, forced me onto it, and strapped me down. Then he stepped back. "I'm sorry, Sam. I truly am. But you did this to yourself. If you'd left well enough alone, you wouldn't be here."

He turned to go.

"He's not taking you with him," I said to his back. He paused. "He's never going to give you the secret of the Philosopher's Stone. You'll never get to suck down some tasty eternal youth or research elementals. He's set you up to take the blame, and he's going to kill you to make sure the blame sticks. Probably get an elemental to do it. Maybe Lorenzo, if he really turns him into a permanent salamander. Burned to death by one of the students you betrayed. Is that what you signed up for?"

"Shut up, Sam," Dr. Ballard said without turning around. He put his hand on the doorknob.

"You said you didn't want all the kids to die," I said, desperately trying to appeal to the teacher I'd always liked. "You've even tried to make them more comfortable here. It's not too late to save them."

He stood there for a second with his hand on the knob, but he didn't answer me. Instead, he went out and closed the door behind him.

I said a bad word, then turned my head to Meg. "So, I hear you're a sylph."

"Yeah. Apparently." She shuddered. "It felt so . . . icky."

"I know," I said.

She stared at me. "You, too?"

"Nymph. Water elemental."

"Great. If we get out of this, we can start our own version of that old band with Lorenzo. Water, Wind & Fire instead of Earth, Wind & Fire."

"Can you sing or play an instrument?"

"No, but I'm totally going to take it up if we escape." She jerked at the straps holding her arms. "Not that that seems likely."

"That's where you're wrong. I can turn into a nymph without his help. And I'll bet you can turn into a sylph on your own, too."

"How?"

I tried to explain to her how it had felt, how I'd found the elemental inside me and forced it out myself, but I didn't really have the words for it and stuttered to a halt. "Just . . . try," I finally said. "Try. We both need to try."

Someone shouted, not far away. "No! Stay away from me!" *Lorenzo!*

"Now!" I yelled, closed my eyes, and tried to repeat what I'd done before.

It worked. In fact, way easier than the first time. One second, I lay on the bed; the next, though my body hadn't moved, I was Sam, the amazing watergirl. I could still see the fiery line of—what had Reiniger called it, "emotional attachment"?—leading to Lorenzo, but I also saw another line, dimmer, less-defined, blue rather than red, but there all the same, leading from me to Meg. She lay with her eyes closed, breathing hard, obviously trying to do what I had told her but without success.

I suddenly had an idea. I mentally took hold of that shining string spanning the space between us and . . . tugged.

It felt like trying to push a car stuck in a snowdrift. At first you can't believe it will ever move, but you rock it, and the wheels keep spinning, and it moves a little bit farther forward every time, and then, suddenly . . .

Sylph-Meg rushed out of her body, a blast of wind that tore spray from my watery form, filling the air with fog for half a second. Then she stood there, invisible except for a slight shimmer in the air. "Meg?" I said in my bubbling nymph voice.

"Sam," she said, her voice a whisper with a low moan to it, like wind in a power line.

"Let's go get Lorenzo," I said.

I followed the fiery line I knew led straight to him.

CHAPTER 24
I MAKE A ROPE

I didn't bother opening the locked door. I went through it as though it were cardboard, smashing it aside with all the strength of my watery body—which was clearly a great deal more than that of my non-watery one. Meg-the-miniature-tornado roared after me, her passage down the hallway ripping a bulletin board off the wall just outside the common room and embedding it in the acoustic tile of the ceiling, smashing a lighting fixture on the way.

As broken glass rained down in her wake, I had to admit, it wasn't exactly a *stealthy* approach. Paracelsus knew we were coming—but only had a couple of seconds' warning before I smashed through the closed door into Lorenzo's room.

Jacqueline must have been just the other side of it: she flew across the room, crashing into Dr. Ballard. They tumbled to the floor together in a tangle of arms and legs and swear words.

Paracelsus, who had his hands on Lorenzo, lying on the bed, turned to face us. "You will *stop*!" he snarled.

For the first time, I felt the force of will Lorenzo had warned me about. It felt like the moment Dr. Ballard had grabbed me from behind up on the surface, except this time, the arms holding me in place were immaterial.

I froze. I couldn't take another step forward.

Unfortunately for him, Paracelsus must not have noticed the nearly invisible Meg-sylph behind me. She roared forward—*through* me, in fact, setting my water body swirling and raising a cloud of mist (if I'd had a stomach, I'm pretty sure I would have thrown up)—and slammed into him. He tumbled backward. In that instant, his hold on me broke, and I hurried toward Lorenzo . . .

. . . who lay on the bed, his eyes open, staring blankly at the ceiling.

Horror filled me. *He's dead!* But no, his bare chest rose and fell, and there was a thin thread of attachment running from me to him. But a second, brighter, thread led . . .

There! Heat and light exploded in the room. Salamander-Lorenzo suddenly appeared behind Paracelsus, who had gotten to his knees but no further. Relief flooded me. He'd attack, he'd . . .

But no. He just stood there, silent, a statue of a boy carved out of flame, and my momentary relief twisted to despair.

The kneeling alchemist's gaze was locked on the swirling shimmer of Meg, whom he clearly held in his control as he had held me a moment before. "One more move from either of you, Sam," he said, never taking his eyes from Meg, "and I will have Lorenzo burn his own body. And then yours and Meg's."

I clenched my watery fists. "You wouldn't."

"Of course, he would, *ma petite,*" said Jacqueline. Having untangled herself from Dr. Ballard, she circled the room to stand beside her husband. "And force you to watch. It might drive you mad, but madness in an elemental is . . . what is the expression? . . . ah, *oui*, a feature, not a bug. And then together, the three of you will be our new servants for however many years your energies persist." She smiled, or at least showed her teeth. "That has always been how this was going to end."

"Please," Dr. Ballard said, his voice soft. "Though I understand they must be sacrificed for the greater good, there's no need to be cruel. They're just children."

"Ah, more of your 'vestigial sympathy,'" Jacqueline said. "Your self-serving prattle fools no one, you pathetic imbecile. You have helped Paracelsus because you wish to be made immortal like him—like *us*. You salved your conscience with your food and toys and cleaning of clothes, but in the end, you are fine with killing children if it means *you* have eternal youth. If you were not, you would never have participated in the charade of the bus crash to begin with."

"You're wrong," Dr. Ballard said. "I'm not involved for myself, but for all of humanity. I want to live only so I can understand how elementals are created, how everyone can benefit from—"

"You will never—"

"Quiet, both of you," said Paracelsus, and maybe they, too, were subject to his force of will because they instantly fell silent. "Let us focus on the immediate problem." Sweat beaded his pale face, and I suddenly realized he was cradling his right arm close to his body. His wrist looked somehow misshapen.

It's broken! It must have happened when Meg hit him. He's in pain. Distracted. And he's struggling just to control Meg. I smiled (though what that looked like on my current face, I had no idea). Meg was a handful for *anyone* to control in sylph *or* human shape. So maybe . . .

"Lorenzo," I called in my weird, bubbling voice. "Can you hear me?"

The fireboy said nothing.

"Lorenzo is gone," Paracelsus snapped. "The salamander belongs to me. You are wasting your time."

You're lying, I thought. *If that were true, you wouldn't bother trying to convince me of it—he'd already be burning all our bodies.*

I looked again at those two threads of attachment, the bright one leading to the fireboy and the much fainter one running to the skinny boy on the bed. I reached out with my mind, just like I had with Meg moments before, and tugged on the thread connecting me to Lorenzo's fire-body as hard as I could.

I felt resistance, but not the same kind as when I'd pulled sylph-Meg out of her body. This felt like a tug of war, me pulling one way, Paracelsus pulling the other. I saw his eyes widen. I pulled harder. He gasped in pain. "No!" he cried. "You can't—"

But I did.

Fire-Lorenzo suddenly rushed toward me, brushing past Paracelsus, who screamed and toppled over onto his left side, away from that blast of heat—freeing Meg.

Rather than take on Paracelsus, who was frantically batting at the smouldering right side of his robe, Meg blasted into Jacqueline just as she pulled her beloved Taser from her pocket. Jacqueline fell backwards into the wall, her skull hitting it with a thump. The Taser clattered onto the floor. She slid down and sat spread-eagled on the floor, looking dazed.

Salamander-Lorenzo had vanished after he swept past me.

Now, real live Lorenzo gulped air, blinked, and sat up. He stared at nymph-me. "Sam?"

"And Meg," I said, nodding to the dust tornado between us and Jacqueline. The fallen Taser came skittering across the floor out of that swirl, hitting my watery toes, which splashed apart and then reformed, which was very weird to see. Not at all sure what electricity would do to me while I was made of water, and not wanting to find out, I hastily stepped to one side.

Paracelsus, robe still smoking slightly, clambered to his feet. Cradling his broken right wrist, he reached out his left hand to Jacqueline and pulled her, wobbling a little, to her feet. She rubbed the back of her head, giving the three of us poisonous looks—though not nearly as poisonous as the one Paracelsus aimed in our direction.

His eyes narrowed. I could feel him gathering his will and braced myself to resist . . . but it wasn't aimed at any of us. "Time to end this. A pity to lose you all, but you are clearly more trouble than you are worth. And Jacqueline and I have already gathered enough life force to buy many more years of youthfulness."

The floor rumbled, shaking my liquid form so hard ripples formed on my surface. "Earth elemental!" I cried— just as the wall behind Paracelsus and Jacqueline collapsed into a mound of broken drywall and crumpled metal. Air rushed from the black tunnel beyond, so cold and fresh it had to be from outside.

Then the elemental itself appeared, splaying its massive mud hands against the edges of the tunnel mouth to pull itself into the room. Meg bravely hurled herself at it but couldn't even stir its surface, doing nothing more than ripping a few dead leaves from it so that, for a moment, I could see her girl-shape marked by their swirling. She fell back.

I knew if I attacked the thing as a nymph, it would simply absorb me into its mud body. Lorenzo had dealt with the earth elemental at my house, but he could do nothing in human form—and if he became a salamander again, Paracelsus might claim him forever.

Paracelsus took Jacqueline's hand. "Farewell," he said. "Hidden in the woods is a car packed with everything we need. You have accomplished nothing."

"Wait!" Dr. Ballard lurched forward from where he had been standing in the corner, back pressed hard against the wall. "You have to take me with you! You said you would—"

"I have said many things to many fools like you over the years," Paracelsus said, voice dripping with contempt. "Idiots enamoured of 'lost knowledge.' Those who fancy themselves witches or warlocks. The greedy. The gullible. The corrupt. Always the same. Always easily enlisted to help. Always easily discarded afterward.

"None of you will leave this place alive, but at least in your case, Ballard, the police will know *why* you disappeared. They will find the handwritten confession I skillfully forged, in which you admit you crashed the bus deliberately and sold the children to human traffickers. They will find large sums of money, matching what you confessed to being paid, deposited to your account from untraceable sources, and the records of the massive gambling debt you accrued over the past several years, against which those sums were applied. And they will find your suicide note, spelling out the immense guilt you suffered because of your reprehensible actions."

"Won't someone notice that *you* vanished?" I said. "You're the vice-principal!"

"Of course not. My dear wife, whom everyone knows has been very ill, has just passed away, and I am taking an extended leave to visit family and grieve. I will not return to the school, of course; I will simply send in a letter of resignation. As you Canadians say, all the bases have been covered. I have been doing this for a very, *very* long time. But I appreciate your concern for my wellbeing . . . considering I have absolutely none for yours." He sighed. "And you *were* a natural . . . the easiest child to turn I have encountered for more than a century." He shook his head. "What a slave you would have made. Pity." He turned to Jacqueline and took her hand. "Come along, *liebchen*."

"*Oui, mon chéri,*" she said.

Together, they disappeared into the tunnel.

The elemental reached inside the tunnel once they had passed it and pulled down the earth above the entrance, blocking it. Then it turned toward us, but it didn't attack; instead, it reached up to rip down the ceiling and the support beams above it.

As dirt thundered down into the room, swirling inside Meg's sylph-body so I could again see her shape clearly, I did what I'd wanted to do earlier: I reached out my watery arms, picked up Lorenzo, and cradled him. With my nymph strength, I barely noticed the weight.

"Meg, back to our bodies!" I yelled.

"You're cold," Lorenzo mumbled. He still seemed a little dazed. "And wet."

"I'm not myself."

Dr. Ballard stood frozen, staring at the elemental. "I can't believe they'd leave me!" he cried.

I told you so, I thought but didn't bother to say as I brushed past him, carrying Lorenzo back to the room where Meg's and my bodies waited. I set Lorenzo on the bed at my body's feet—he looked a little more awake—then undid the straps holding my body to the bed. Only then did I let the growing need to be back in my own flesh suck me back into it.

I gasped, opened my real eyes, pulled my hands and legs free of the straps, got up, and gave Lorenzo a real hug. "Warmer now?" I said.

"Yes," he said, hugging me back. He released me as I stepped back. "What now?"

"We have to get everyone out." Rumbling sounds continued down the hall. "But they're all so weak! Meg and I can't . . ."

"I'll help," said Dr. Ballard, coming into the room, face pale. "I know where everyone is."

I nodded, too furious at him to speak.

"Come help me, Meg," he said. She scowled but followed him out of the room.

Lorenzo struggled to his feet. I put his arm over my shoulders. While I helped him down the hallway and across the common room, Meg and Dr. Ballard began opening doors and freeing children, most of whom seemed to be in the dorm wing.

I left Lorenzo at the bottom of the stairs, then went to free Melanie from the rec room. She cried when she saw me.

Everyone was dressed the same, girls in hospital gowns, boys in pyjama bottoms. Everyone was skinny. All were weak, although none were as weak as Lorenzo, so at least they could walk. We got them all to the stairs while the rumbling sounds of destruction grew louder and louder, like an approaching thunderstorm.

That storm burst into the common room just as we started helping kids up the first flight of stairs to the hallway leading to the staircase to the surface. The far wall erupted as the elemental burst through. He grabbed the nearest pillar and tore it from its footing, and a large chunk of the ceiling collapsed around him, crushing one of the old round tables beneath it.

We got everyone up into the hallways and down them to the main staircase. Together, we started the laborious climb. Some of the kids, using the railing, managed the ascent on their own, step by torturous step. Others, including Lorenzo and Melanie, we had to help. Behind us, we heard enormous rumbles and crashes, and we were buffeted by blasts of dank, musty, locker-room-scented air.

"He must have . . . pre-programmed . . . that elemental to destroy the place," Dr. Ballard panted on his way up the stairs. He was helping Melanie, and I was close behind with Lorenzo, bringing up the rear. "It's probably the same one that brought down the landslide over the garage doors. He thought everyone would already be dead when he triggered it, or he would have started the destruction at this end."

"Lucky he didn't," I gasped as we reached the top flight of the stairs. My other classmates sat slumped on the steps. Dr. Ballard helped Meg sit down on one, and I lowered Lorenzo onto another.

"Thanks," he said faintly.

I gave him a quick grin, then picked my way through the other kids up to the top, where Meg and Dr. Ballard already stood.

"Really glad I decided to talk to you the day you showed up in my backyard," Meg said to me. "It's been nothing but fun ever since."

"What can I say?" I replied. "Fun is my middle name."

Dr. Ballard pushed open the door, throwing it up and over so that it crashed against its concrete frame. Cold air flooded down the steps. Dr. Ballard followed that icy draft down the stairs to start helping kids up them while Meg and I climbed up and out, then turned to pull the others out as they reached us.

One by one, the members of my Grade 7 science class emerged onto the meadow's damp grass. The first kid I helped was my old nemesis, Nick, though I hardly recognized him: he definitely didn't look like a buff athlete anymore. He took my proffered hand numbly as he stepped out into the clearing. "Thanks, Sam," he said. There were tears in his eyes. I seemed to have something in my eyes, too.

I found myself blinking and sniffling a lot as each of my rescued classmates appeared in the doorway. Melanie. Pyotr. Anna Lockwood. Sammy Starblanket. Gursh Patel. Laura-Ann Gilbert. Zhao Yifei, all the others—my friends I'd thought were gone forever, children whose parents and siblings thought they were gone forever; who *would* have been gone forever if Paracelsus and the evil Jacqueline had had their way, entombed by the elemental whose labours below us shook the ground beneath my feet.

"We need to get out of the compound," Dr. Ballard said, emerging last, behind Lorenzo, who seemed to be getting stronger: he'd managed to climb the steps himself and gave me a grin, a pale imitation of his old one, but a grin nonetheless, as he took my hand and let me pull him out. A blast of foul air suddenly gusted out of the door around Dr. Ballard, and the ground shook even more. "If the whole bunker collapses, we could all—"

He never finished. Behind him, on the rise where his camp

still stood, something rose in the darkness, something man-shaped but much larger. The pale shape of Dr. Ballard's tent vanished, swallowed by the earth. I was pretty sure my backpack, left behind when I entered the bunker, had just joined it.

"Another elemental!" I screamed, pointing.

Dr. Ballard spun, took one look, shouted, "Run, Sam! Get everyone out!"—and then, to my utter astonishment, dashed toward the looming creature.

I don't know what he thought he could do against a mass of living mud twice as tall as he was. Maybe it was that "vestigial sympathy" Jacqueline had mocked him for. I think that somewhere in his mind, he remembered that he was our teacher, responsible for our safety. Yes, he was equally responsible for having put us all into this horrible danger to begin with, and in the end, when he'd learned what Paracelsus really intended for us, he'd given in rather than try to stand up to him. But all the same . . . *this* time, he ran toward the danger threatening us.

He took something from his coat and raised it—a pistol, I realized. It spat fire with a flat cracking sound that echoed back from the hillside above us.

He couldn't have missed at that range. But he might as well have fired the bullet into the ground for all the good it did. The elemental responded with a sweeping backhand that lifted Dr. Ballard off the ground and hurled him fifty feet through the air like a rag doll thrown by a child. He hit the ground hard, with a horrible crunching thud, and didn't move again.

I glanced over my shoulder. Meg was trying to herd the kids away from the elemental, but most of them had collapsed to the ground, what little strength they had utterly spent from the effort of climbing the stairs. I spun around again. Though it had paused to deal with Dr. Ballard, the elemental was walking toward us—very slowly, like a man wading through thick muck, but then, it didn't have far to go. It would reach us in seconds.

Maybe if I turn into a nymph, I could . . .

But I knew it was hopeless, as hopeless as it had been when the first earth elemental had appeared down in the bunker—and that one had been a lot smaller than this one. The thing would absorb my water form into its earth-body an instant, and squash my prostrate body like a bug a second later.

I stood frozen, indecisive, out of ideas. Meg and I might be able to outrun the thing, but the others—

Light blossomed, red and bright, behind me, and warmth touched my skin. I gasped and spun. "Lorenzo, no—"

There he stood, the fireboy, his thin human body sprawled senseless on the ground at his feet. He didn't say anything to me. He rushed past in a blast of heat and light, and I twisted around again to see him hurl himself against one of the elemental's massive legs.

There, he blazed, bright and hot as a cutting torch. Steam and acrid smoke exploded, and the thing toppled, roaring, as its leg crumbled beneath it. It managed a swipe at Lorenzo as it fell, but its giant fist passed harmlessly through his flame, barely even disrupting his boy shape—which then leaped onto the thing's head. There was another explosion of steam and muck and acrid smoke and the decapitated elemental suddenly became nothing more than a slumping pile of dirt.

Fire-Lorenzo stood atop that pile, not moving, not speaking. He stared at me briefly with bright, blank eyes . . . and then turned and started to walk away from all of us, away from his body, dimming with each step.

No! I thought. *No! His body will die! He'll be an elemental forever . . .*

No!

I had to stop him, and there was nothing I could do in my flesh-and-blood body.

So I left it.

It collapsed onto the ground, falling from my nymph form like a discarded bathrobe. I hoped I hadn't broken anything in it. But that seemed unimportant. Only Lorenzo mattered . . . and the thin line of fire that still joined us, though it grew thinner with every step he took, dwindling as he moved away from me.

I wanted to pull on it as I had before, stop him, yank him back to me, back to his body, before it was too late . . . but I could sense, knew without a doubt, that the thread between us was too fragile for that now. In moments, it would snap completely, and Lorenzo would be lost forever.

So I did the only other thing I could think of: I poured *myself* into that thread, all the affection and friendship I'd felt for Lorenzo for so many years, every day of tobogganing or skating, every night lying in our backyards looking up at the stars, every board game and homework night and recess, all the days of biking and swimming and playing in the woods, and most of all, all the hours of talking, about everything and nothing, some of it profound (at least to us), some of it inconsequential. I had loved it all, and so had he.

The thread grew brighter under that torrent of love, brighter and thicker, until it wasn't a thread anymore; it was a strong rope, a cable, a chain strong enough to anchor the *Titanic*. Then, and only then, I pulled at it with my mind . . .

. . . and Lorenzo came, resistance fading almost at once, as though he were a boat I were pulling into a dock. He didn't rush toward me like he had down below but walked step by step. For a moment, we faced each other, watergirl and fireboy. "Thank you," he said, his voice a crackling whisper.

"Any time," I said, my own voice the burble of a mountain stream.

Then the fireboy vanished, and the real boy stiffened, arched his back, and gasped, a huge intake of air, followed by coughing, followed by his getting onto his hands and knees and retching.

Only then did I drop my nymph form and fall back into my body, which also gasped and then said, "Ow," because apparently when I'd let my body fall, it had plunked its . . . my . . . rear end onto a sizable rock. Nausea rolled inside me, too, for a moment, but I swallowed hard, and it subsided.

I rolled off the rock onto my hands and knees, gave my sore rump a rub, and then crawled across the damp grass to Lorenzo, who had rolled over onto his back again and was staring up at the sky. I gave him a look like a cat in the morning, wondering if its owner was awake yet. "Are you all right?"

He blinked at me. "No," he said, his voice a pale, whispering ghost of what it should have been. "But I think . . . I will be."

The ground rumbled beneath us. I remembered the other elemental down there, tearing the bunker apart piece by piece. I looked up to see Meg looking down at Lorenzo and me, her smile verging just a little too close to a smirk for my taste. I scrambled to my feet. "We need to get away from here," I told her. "There's a place at the back of the compound where the fence is . . ." but then my voice trailed off as I looked at the sad collection of near-starved children slumped cross-legged or stretched out full length on the ground behind her. There was no way they were getting out the way I'd come in.

Remembering how I'd had to jump over the barbed wire at the top of the tilted-over fence when I'd entered the compound, I wasn't sure I could get out that way, either.

"Better to go the other way," Meg said. "Follow the fence to the front of the compound. Then you or I can head out to the road and flag down a car."

"What if the cops padlocked the gate?"

"Then you or I will tear it open." She grinned at me. "Elementals, remember?"

I laughed a little weakly. "You wouldn't think I could forget." I glanced at where Dr. Ballard had landed. "Is he . . .?"

Meg swallowed and nodded. "I . . . checked."

I felt bad. He really had been my favourite teacher. And trying to save us, here at the end, had been really brave. Maybe it didn't make up for what he'd done to land us all here in the first place, but it was still really brave.

Without Dr. Ballard, it was up to Meg and me to help everyone else out to the front of the compound. The rumbling and shaking continued, and now big clouds of dust were exploding at regular intervals out of the door we'd escaped through, just visible in the starlight.

It took multiple trips, but eventually, we had everyone on the flat ground in front of the buried garage doors. My bare feet felt numb with cold, and my barely-dressed body was one giant goose bump by the time we were done. The other kids were so weak and sick I was afraid some of them might die of exposure before we could get help, so we had everyone lie down close beside each other to share body heat.

We gave the buried bunker a wide berth, and a good

thing, too: ten minutes after we got everyone clear, the rumbling rose to a roar, and the slab of concrete buried beneath the elemental-created landslide that had hidden the garage doors suddenly lifted into the air and slid forward, hitting the ground with an earth-shaking thud. A huge cloud of dust rolled over us, leaving us coughing—but the cold night breeze quickly cleared it away.

After that, deathly silence hung over the compound.

I didn't want to leave Lorenzo, so Meg climbed up the hill to check out the front gate, reappearing at the top a moment after she disappeared to shout back that the gate was still open and she was heading to the road to flag down help.

She vanished, and I joined the huddle of kids on the ground, curled up together like a litter of abandoned puppies. At some point, with my arms around Lorenzo, I dozed off.

I woke to the sound of sirens, and shortly after that, the grown-ups took over.

One was my father. He didn't ask me any questions; he just wrapped me in his warm arms and hugged me like he'd never let me go.

Right then, I hoped he never would.

CHAPTER 25
I SUGGEST WE GO FOR HOT DOGS

Two weeks later, I, Meg, and a still very skinny Lorenzo sat on a rock in Peterson Park, up a hill just outside of Limberpine, looking down at the town. From there, we could see all of downtown, plus the school, The Dog Pound, Meg's house, Lorenzo's house, and the apartment building where Paracelsus had once lurked. Only my house, currently surrounded by scaffolding, was out of sight, hidden on the far side of town.

It had been a crazy couple of weeks. There had been joy and grief as parents and families were reunited with their missing children. My hatred for Paracelsus and Jacqueline flared up in me again as I thought about what all those families had gone through.

The circling media vultures had, of course, dropped down on us again, fighting each other over scavenged bits of information. None of the kids who had been locked up had any idea of what had been going on. Even though I knew Paracelsus had turned other kids than just us three into elementals, it seemed like after he left, they'd forgotten. A lot of the kids seemed kind of confused about what had happened—some side effect of his powers, I guess.

But the three of us, who had learned to turn ourselves into elementals—we remembered. We remembered *everything*.

We were the only three who knew that Vice-Principal Reiniger and his wife had been behind the whole thing. We made sure he got as much blame as we could attach to him, although the forged letters and other evidence he'd left behind thoroughly implicated the late Dr. Ballard. The story of middle-school teachers who had sold their students to human traffickers found fertile ground in the media—even though nobody could quite figure out what the point had been of keeping the kids locked up and gradually starving to death. The best explanation anyone had come up with was that the buyers had backed out and they'd been trying to find new ones while lacking the resources to keep the kids in good shape.

Teachers selling students to traffickers was such a horrifying idea it sucked up all of CBC's attention for days. The Prime Minister made a speech. The Opposition weighed in. There was talk of new legislation . . .

And only Lorenzo, Meg, and I knew the truth. Only we knew Reiniger had really been Paracelsus. And only we knew that he was still out there with his she-devil wife, Jacqueline and that sooner or later, another group of children would be taken, twisted, and sucked dry of life.

We couldn't tell anyone. Who would believe us?

Oh, sure, we could have turned into elementals right in front of them. But we'd all read the books and seen the movies about kids with special powers, and this time, I thought they were probably right. In stories, kids like that are either a) locked up and studied, b) turned into super-soldiers, or c) deemed dangerous and made to disappear.

No, thanks. No way we were telling *anyone* what we could do.

That didn't mean, of course, that we weren't going to do it.

We looked at each other, went around to the far side of the rock, and lay down on the ground, side by side.

A minute later, we stood on the rock again, but now we were a boy carved from flame, a girl made of water, and a swirling, whispering disturbance in the air.

"Water, Wind & Fire," I reminded Meg in my bubbling voice.

"I still can't play an instrument," the whirlwind whispered.

"And I still can't sing," crackled the fireboy.

I looked with my nymph mind at the bright lines of attachment between us, the fiery red one between me and Lorenzo, the blue one between me and Meg. I couldn't see the purple one between Meg and Lorenzo, but they'd both told me it was there. "So we'll learn," I said.

"School starts tomorrow," the fireboy said.

"Two weeks late," I burbled. Apparently, losing two teachers just before the school year had caused some staffing issues.

"Still too soon," said the whirlwind.

"I wonder who our new science teacher will be?" crackled the fireboy.

I turned to face my real body, lying behind the rock between Lorenzo's and Meg's. "Let's go back to the Dog Pound, stuff our faces with cylindrical meat byproducts, and talk about it."

The whirlwind and the fireboy laughed.

Five minutes later, we were on our bikes, headed down the hill, just three ordinary friends enjoying the evening, glad to be alive.

Our route took us past the school. I glanced at it on the way by.

One thing's for sure, I thought. *It's going to be an interesting year.*

ABOUT EDWARD WILLETT

Edward Willett is the award-winning author (under his own name and as E.C. Blake and Lee Arthur Chane) of more than sixty books of science fiction, fantasy, and nonfiction for readers of all ages, including twelve novels for DAW Books. He has been short-listed multiple times for Saskatchewan Book Awards, and won for his young adult fantasy *Spirit Singer* (Shadowpaw Press). He won Canada's top science fiction and fantasy award, the Aurora, for his second novel for DAW, *Marseguro*, and has been shortlisted several times since, including for his most recent young adult science fiction novel, *Star Song* (Shadowpaw Press). Ed has also won an Aurora Award for his podcast, *The Worldshapers*. In addition to being a writer and editor, Ed is a professional actor and singer. He lives in Regina, Saskatchewan, with his wife, Margaret Anne Hodges, a professional engineer.

ABOUT SHADOWPAW PRESS

Shadowpaw Press is a small traditional publishing company located in Regina, Saskatchewan, Canada, founded in 2018 by Edward Willett, an award-winning author of science fiction, fantasy, and non-fiction for readers of all ages. A member of Literary Press Group (Canada) and the Association of Canadian Publishers, it publishes an eclectic selection of books, including adult fiction, young adult fiction, children's books, non-fiction, and anthologies.

You can find Shadowpaw Press online at shadowpawpress.com or on Facebook, Instagram, or X @shadowpawpress. Email publisher@shadowpawpress.com for more information.

MORE BOOKS FOR YOUNG READERS

Picture Books

The Wind and Amanda's Cello

by Alison Lohans, illustrated by Sarah Shortliffe

Middle-Grade Books

Stay by Katherine Lawrence

The Canadian Chills series by Arthur Slade

Young Adult Books

The Headmasters by Mark Morton

The Sun Runners by James Bow

The Night Girl by James Bow

The Emir's Falcon by Matt Hughes

Blue Fire by E. C. Blake

The Ghosts of Spiritwood by Martine Noël-Maw

Star Song

Spirit Singer

From the Street to the Stars

The Shards of Excalibur Series

Soulworm

by Edward Willett